W9-BYN-870

"I've Changed My Mind," Rocky Said. "I Want To Leave."

"You wouldn't make it down the stairs without collapsing." Worth lifted the boy into his arms and strode straight for his bathroom. Seating his unwilling guest on the counter, he turned to fill the tub. "Since you won't let me take you to the hospital, the least I can do is clean you up before I drive you home."

Satisfied things were under way, Worth backed out of the room. "I'll be out here. If you need anything, yell."

Closing the door behind him, he shut his eyes and shook his head. Then he heard the crash. The scream. The splash.

He raced for the bathroom, threw open the door and—and stared incredulously at the horrified young *woman* in his bathtub. The *naked* young woman in his bathtub...

Dear Reader,

We here at Silhouette Desire just couldn't resist bringing you another special theme month. Have you ever wondered what it is about our heroes that enables them to win the heroines' love? Of course, these men have undeniable sex appeal, and they have charm (loads of it!), and even if they're rough around the edges, you know that, deep down, they have tender hearts.

In a way, their magnetism, their charisma, is simply indescribable. These men are . . . simply Irresistible! This month, we think we've picked six heroes who are going to knock your socks off! And when these six irresistible men meet six *very* unattainable women, passion flares, sparks fly—and *you* get hours of reading pleasure!

And what month would be complete without a terrific *Man of the Month?* Delightful Dixie Browning has created a man to remember in Stone McCloud, the hero of *Lucy and the Stone. Man of the Month* fun just keeps on coming in upcoming months, with exciting love stories by Jackie Merritt, Joan Hohl, Barbara Boswell, Annette Broadrick, Lass Small and a *second* 1994 *Man of the Month* book by Ann Major.

So don't miss a single Silhouette Desire book! And, until next month, happy reading from . . .

Lucia Macro
Senior Editor

Please address questions and book requests to:
Reader Service
U.S.: P.O. Box 1325, Buffalo, NY 14269
Canadian: P.O. Box 1050, Niagara Falls, Ont. L2E 7G7

HELEN R. MYERS

ONCE UPON A FULL MOON

SILHOUETTE *Desire*®

Published by Silhouette Books

America's Publisher of Contemporary Romance

If you purchased this book without a cover you should be aware that this book is stolen property. It was reported as "unsold and destroyed" to the publisher, and neither the author nor the publisher has received any payment for this "stripped book."

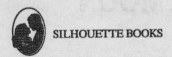

SILHOUETTE BOOKS

ISBN 0-373-05857-8

ONCE UPON A FULL MOON

Copyright © 1994 by Helen R. Myers

All rights reserved. Except for use in any review, the reproduction or utilization of this work in whole or in part in any form by any electronic, mechanical or other means, now known or hereafter invented, including xerography, photocopying and recording, or in any information storage or retrieval system, is forbidden without the written permission of the editorial office, Silhouette Books, 300 East 42nd Street, New York, NY 10017 U.S.A.

All characters in this book have no existence outside the imagination of the author and have no relation whatsoever to anyone bearing the same name or names. They are not even distantly inspired by any individual known or unknown to the author, and all incidents are pure invention.

This edition published by arrangement with Harlequin Enterprises B. V.

® and TM are trademarks of Harlequin Enterprises B. V., used under license. Trademarks indicated with ® are registered in the United States Patent and Trademark Office, the Canadian Trade Marks Office and in other countries.

Printed in U.S.A.

Books by Helen R. Myers

Silhouette Desire

Partners for Life #370
Smooth Operator #454
That Fontaine Woman! #471
The Pirate O'Keefe #506
Kiss Me Kate #570
After You #599
When Gabriel Called #650
Navarrone #738
Jake #797
Once Upon a Full Moon #857

Silhouette Romance

Donovan's Mermaid #557
Someone To Watch Over Me #643
Confidentially Yours #677
Invitation to a Wedding #737
A Fine Arrangement #776
Through My Eyes #814
Three Little Chaperones #861
Forbidden Passion #908
A Father's Promise #1002

Silhouette Shadows

Night Mist #6
Whispers in the Woods #23

Silhouette Books

Silhouette Shadows Short Story Collection 1992
"Seawitch"

HELEN R. MYERS

satisfies her preference for a reclusive life-style by living deep in the Piney Woods of East Texas with her husband, Robert, and—because they were there first—the various species of four-legged and winged creatures that wander throughout their ranch. To write has been her lifelong dream, and to bring a slightly different flavor to each book is an ongoing ambition.

One

"I'm sorry, Worth. It's over."

For seconds after the line went dead, he sat behind his desk, telephone receiver in hand, staring into his dark office. It wasn't hurt he had to adjust to—he'd never lied to Erica by suggesting he loved her—it was simple astonishment.

So that's what she'd been up to during her European holiday. Erica Landon, the woman he'd been seeing for two years, give or take a few months, had just dumped him for Werner Strassel, the German banker who was showing up in all the business magazines as the most successful deal maker with Eastern Block countries since the Wall came down.

Strassel, of all people! The guy had to be a dozen years older than Worth's own thirty-six and more than a few umlauts shorter than his solid six feet. What's more, every press photo Worth had seen of him betrayed the fact that the financial baron had a weakness for his fatherland's famous lager. Of course, Worth knew looks had nothing to do with Erica's decision. No, it was the extra zero on the billionaire's financial statement that had done it. He was convinced.

"Exactly how much is rich enough?" he snapped at the silent phone.

Disgusted, he slammed the handset back onto the cradle. Fine. If she wanted old Werner the Marksmaker, she could have him. No one dropped Worth Harrison Drury IV as a method of stirring *his* jealousy.

But this did put him in unfamiliar territory.

Up until now he'd always been the one to sever a relationship, once he'd ascertained it was a dead-end type of situation where anything more, specifically marriage, was out of the question. Most of the time it took only a few dates to determine that. In Erica's case it had taken almost two years. He supposed that explained why he felt offended. Truth be known, he had begun to see the possibility of spending the rest of his life with her. They'd been compatible on so many levels.

Or so he'd believed.

"I know what you're thinking, but it's not merely money. I'm marrying Werner because he knows what the word romance *means, Worth. Romance* and *passion."*

Romance. He snorted. Since when had she preferred sentimentality over diamonds or a new sports car? And hadn't she told him that his levelheaded, clear-sighted approach to relationships was refreshing and a relief to her?

As for *passion*... He could show her a thing or two about passion. Why, at this very moment he would happily sacrifice the sum total of his quarterly dividends for thirty seconds with his hands around that conniving witch's neck!

No, she wasn't going to ease her conscience by insinuating he'd been indifferent to her emotional needs. She'd finally shown her true colors, exactly as the others had; precisely as he predicted *all* women did sooner or later. She was a selfish, greedy piranha, who'd found herself a bigger pond to feast in. As far as he was concerned, she'd done him a favor, and she could have her honeymoon in the lobby of Strassel's favorite Swiss bank for all he cared.

Women. Why did he continue to bother with them? Despite making things clear from the onset about how he didn't believe in empty declarations of love or public displays of affection, that he felt a lasting relationship came from mutual respect and understanding, every woman he'd ever dated had, sooner or later, tried to change him into exactly the kind of pandering, placating sop he abhorred.

Enough was enough. He was through with the lot of them. The woman didn't exist for whom he would bend his own rules. Let Chase, who was already making a career out of tarnishing the family name with his impetuous liaisons, have the privilege of sifting through the masses.

Expelling his irritation in one purging breath, Worth leaned back into the soft leather of his chair and shifted his gaze to the crystal sculpture on the corner of his desk. Focusing on *Galatea* always eased his agitation. Tonight, however, she caused an odd twist deep inside him, too. An increasingly familiar one.

The first time he'd experienced it was when he'd passed a quaint, dusty shop and spotted her in the window. He'd felt... the sensation had been one of surprise to find a contemporary piece among mostly antiques... and yearning; a yearning he'd been hiding from the world, from people, who—if they'd ever discovered it—would undoubtedly use the knowledge to manipulate, if not de-

stroy him. As far as he was concerned, he'd had no choice
but to buy her.

Everyone who saw her complimented him on his eye for
value. Only his precious figurine knew the real reason he
had to have the piece or why he experienced such a hunger
when he caressed her. It wasn't because of her worth as an
investment, but because he could not find her human
likeness anywhere.

He had to learn to stop trying.

Worth turned away from her. He couldn't let himself
touch her tonight. He was too angry. Too disappointed in
himself. Too disappointed with life in general.

Abruptly he pushed himself to his feet and checked his
pockets for his car keys. Also too wired to stay here any
longer, he decided that if he slipped out the back way, he
could avoid the rest of Drury Development, Inc.'s annual
Christmas party, which was going on in the main office.
His father and Chase could handle things. Neither his
brother nor W.H. would miss him. What's more, both
made far more enthusiastic toastmasters than he would
ever be.

He wanted the privacy of his own four walls. No doubt
McGuire had already lit a fire in the study fireplace. In
fact, the first thing he would do when he reached his car
would be to phone his man. He wanted McGuire to clear
away all evidence of the intimate dinner he'd planned to
share with Erica upon her arrival from the airport.

Yes, a call would save him from having to deal with
some of his servant's cartoonish expressions and irreverent editorializing. Especially the remarks Worth knew
would be voiced once McGuire learned Erica not only
wasn't coming to dinner but was staying in Europe. Although an efficient butler and a splendid cook, Mc-

Guire's aptitude for maintaining the deportment of a traditional servant left something to be desired.

On the other hand, Buckingham Palace's loss had proved his gain. If the Englishman had been more successful at containing himself, McGuire would still be attending the royals, and Worth would be looking elsewhere for someone to cater to his own discerning needs.

He sighed. Yes, a call would alleviate unnecessary aggravation. Then, as soon as he arrived at home, he could pour himself a drink, settle down in his favorite chair and spend the rest of the evening enjoying a beloved Beethoven CD. His spirits lifted. Erica had disliked the composer's work, replacing the recordings at every opportunity with a more sentimental Chopin or an elusive Debussy.

Tonight he wanted the power and reliable solidity of Beethoven. Beethoven, he wished he could point out to his ex-lover, had been a composer who had possessed *real* passion.

Women. Bah.

Barely ten minutes later Worth was easing his imported sedan through the emptying streets of midtown Boston. Between the full moon and the holiday lights adorning everything, the city had a surreal look. It hardly seemed eight o'clock in the evening.

He finished his call to McGuire as he pulled up to a red traffic light. A couple emerged from a restaurant and stepped into the night, Christmas music floating out with them. Worth found the joyful melody and their laughter as disagreeable as the frigid air lingering in his car. He ducked deeper into the upturned collar of his cashmere coat, as much to escape the wintery cold as to block out the sound and sight of their happiness.

He would bet anything that by next week they would be bickering and grumbling about bills, babies and budgets. So much for romance and passion.

After turning right at the next intersection, he traveled down a less brightly lit street. His thoughts shifted to the package waiting for Erica at his brownstone. The diamond bracelet, elegantly wrapped by his favorite jeweler, matched the earrings he'd given her for her birthday.

It would have to be sent back.

Worth pressed his lips together. He disliked returning things, even when forced by a situation out of his control. It made him feel as though his decision-making processes were...flawed. He objected to even the slightest inference that he'd been wrong about something. About anything. He worked too hard at avoiding errors, at being correct.

At least he'd been smart enough not to hand over her Christmas present early, despite her none-too-subtle hinting for it weeks ago. The conniving little... Had she been planning this elopement with Strassel even then? Worth's grip tightened on the steering wheel and he accelerated, more eager than ever to get home. If that Jezebel believed she could have kept the bracelet once she'd announced her treasonous act, she would have been in for an unpleasant discovery. As a matter of fact he wouldn't have hesitated to—

"Damn!"

The figure shot out of the darkness and dashed in front of his car. Worth jerked the steering wheel to the left, trying to cut behind the fellow. At the same time he slammed on the brakes. Fortunately there was no oncoming traffic.

But he also realized he could have driven the brake pedal through the floorboard and it wouldn't have done any good. Impact was unavoidable.

The horrible thud of steel striking human flesh and bone had him stiffening against a surge of revulsion. Fleetingly he glimpsed a small, pale face... then the boy went flying, a blurred projectile disappearing into the darkness.

The car jerked to a halt. Worth downshifted, set the flashers and then leapt from the car.

Where was he? Parked vehicles lined both sides of the road, making it difficult to spot his victim.

Victim... oh, God.

Then he heard the groan.

He raced toward the sound and spotted the prone figure stuffed halfway under a delivery truck. Worth crouched by the vehicle's bumper, his heart pounding in his throat and every limb. "How bad are you hurt, son?"

After an abrupt sob, he heard, "Stupid, sorry son of a—" The rest of his epithet became a grinding of clenched teeth.

The kid was hurting, but at least he could talk. "Easy," Worth soothed. "Everything's going to be all right."

"Get away from me, you... you... *moron.*"

While disconcerted over what could come out of the mouths of adolescents these days, the youngster's verbal assault wasn't nearly as offensive to Worth as the odor from what he was lying in. The boy had landed by an alley, and whatever some shopkeeper had seen fit to hose out of his back door, it hadn't quite made it to the sewer drain a few yards away.

"I know you're in pain and that I scared the hell out of you," Worth said, guilt giving him more tolerance for rudeness than usual. "But what's important right now is to get you out of that mess. Can you manage to slide from there on your own?"

"Not with you blocking my way."

Repressing his exasperation, Worth shifted back into the road slightly. As soon as the boy began to move, he reached out to help him. "Watch your head!" he blurted out. But too late. With a resounding thump, the youngster's head came in hard contact with the truck's rusty bumper.

"Ow! Why don't you—" The rest of the insult—an innovative suggestion wholly new to Worth and no doubt physically impossible—ended with the boy pressing his face into the filthy, wet sleeve of a jacket that, even in the dark, looked several sizes too big for him.

Worth winced, but didn't quite know how to respond. He could remember well how he'd felt as a teenager when he'd hurt himself, and tears had stung in his eyes. It wasn't a time for having people fuss over you, especially a mature man. At least the boy had been wearing a heavy knit cap. Maybe it had provided more protection than he'd guessed and hadn't broken the skin.

"Come on," he coaxed, "try again."

"Get lost, will ya."

If only he could. He would like nothing better. If only he'd stayed at the party.

Deciding the only way to accomplish anything was to get the boy's mind off the pain, Worth drawled, "Absolutely. And gladly. That is, once you haul your offensive young self out from under there."

"What did you call me?"

"I want to reassure myself that a negligent upbringing is the only thing you're suffering from."

"Pig."

"Interesting summation, my friend, considering you're the one soaking in swill."

The tactic worked. It took a while, and the boy stifled several moans and gasps in the process, but he finally made his way from beneath the truck.

Another vehicle slowed and then accelerated past them. Worth paid it little attention. While this was still one of the reasonably safe parts of town, nightfall changed everything. Despite it being Christmas Eve, people were not apt to involve themselves in other people's problems.

The reminder of the holiday had him feeling guilty again. He had to remind himself of how much worse things could have turned out.

As the boy rolled to a sitting position, Worth had his first front view of him—a privilege he could have done without.

The boy looked a fright. No fashion plate to begin with, he thought, eyeing ragged sneakers, ripped jeans, threadbare plaid jacket and a knit cap, now everything was also drenched with slimy, grayish-brown . . . sludge.

"How are you?" Worth asked him, feeling a wholly new dismay.

"Mental midget, how d'ya think I am?"

"I meant, can you tell if anything's broken?"

"Whadda you care? Afraid I'm gonna sue? I should, y'know, since you was speeding and all."

"I wasn't speeding," Worth replied, maintaining his polite demeanor, although a warning bell sounded inside him. All he needed was this young roughneck to be the sort who sniffed money the way a starving pup sniffed a free meal. "And you had no business running across the street without first checking for traffic. How old are you anyway?"

"None of your business."

Young. He sighed. "All I'm trying to impress upon you is how grateful we should be. Things could have turned out much worse."

"I got all the impressions I need, buster. I'm the one who got hit, remember?"

"Think of the Christmas your family would have had to face if you'd been seriously hurt."

"You're breaking my heart."

He'd used his best business voice, the one that normally had corporate attorneys advising clients to reevaluate their positions, take the money and run. He should have known punks, even ones this young, responded better to muscle than reasoning.

"Okay, my friend, have it your way." Without further warning, he took hold of the back of the boy's collar and hoisted him to his feet. "Let me enlighten you about a few things. One is that this hasn't been the best day of my life, either. What's more, you are, without a doubt, the most foul-mouthed little fiend that I've ever had the misfortune to meet. Now, although I deeply regret what's happened, in case you haven't noticed, this *wasn't* a hit-and-run. So how about a modicum of cooperation, hmm?"

He thought his was an admirable effort in restraint, and even though he felt a shudder race through the kid—who, he concluded, wouldn't weigh more than a hundred pounds when stripped of the rags and street filth—Worth assumed he'd cut through all that posturing nonsense and had reached a clear line of communication. What he hadn't considered was that the boy was seriously hurt. Realization came the moment he released his hold.

His victim collapsed faster than a business deal gone sour, hitting the wet pavement with a hoarse cry. Feeling like something lower than a slug, Worth followed. That's when he noticed the larger tear in the boy's ragged jeans . . . his ripped, raw knee . . . and the blood. The sight of the latter had him thinking about how the youngster had been lying under the truck, exposed to the filth in the gutter.

Worth shuddered. "For the love of heaven . . . I asked if you were hurt!"

The boy didn't answer at first. He was too preoccupied with hugging his injured limb and rocking back and forth. But Worth could see his profile and how his features were twisted into a grimace of pain. If he hadn't been certain the kid would take a swing at him, he would have rubbed the poor tyke's back or squeezed his shoulder in compassion.

"There must be someone I can call for you?" He surprised himself with how much kindness he heard in his voice. "I have a phone in the car."

"No."

"How about 911?"

"Can't you just get outta my face!" the boy growled.

This was what babies grew into, Worth thought with an inner sigh. And yet his father continued to lobby for grandchildren. "Believe me, there's nothing I'd like more. Unfortunately, I have to live with my conscience." With a last glance at the boy's filthy condition, he made his decision. "All right, then. If you won't let me get help for you, I'm going to put you in my car and drive you to the hospital myself."

"No hospital!"

So far the kid's voice had been low and belligerent, making it difficult to pinpoint his age, but now it rose to that crackling level that had Worth guessing he could be dealing with someone at the lower range of his initial estimation. Surely not much more than thirteen, he concluded, glancing at a bony knee and almost dainty-size feet.

That flashed a different nightmare before his eyes, namely the headline this could make: Boston Mogul Flattens Runt of Litter. Family Suit Throws Drury Dynasty into Bankruptcy Court.

"I assure you," he added dryly, "I'll be covering your expenses."

"No hospital."

Worth tapped his fingers against his far sturdier knee. Exactly who did this midget hellion think he was?

"All right," he said, drawing the words out as he struggled to come up with other options. There were pitiful few. "Then I'll drive you home."

"Uh-uh. No way."

"This is not something that's up for debate."

"Forget it. I ain't from this neighborhood."

It took all of Worth's control not to correct the boy's grammar. "A few blocks here or there isn't a problem."

"Mister, d'you need me to spell it out for you?"

"Any respectable form of English would do."

The boy narrowed his eyes. "You go to my neighborhood and you'll do good to leave, with your fancy-smancy accent."

What accent? As the boy sniffed and wiped his runny nose in his sleeve, Worth shut his eyes and considered asking the gods what he'd done to deserve all this. "Please don't do that."

"Do what?"

It was almost funny. If this whole mess of a situation had begun on a less dangerous note, and if he'd been in a better place mentally, he might have laughed. As it was, he thought he did well to merely mutter, "Never mind. Just understand this—I'm not leaving you until we get you cleaned up and somewhere safer than the street. Got it? At the least I intend to phone your parents and let them know what's happened."

"You can't."

"Why not? Aren't they at home?"

"Yeah . . . something like that."

The mumbled reply was as poignant as what his words suggested. Worth exhaled carefully. He didn't want to sound pitying. He'd already figured out the boy didn't respond well to anything that might be misconstrued as patronization.

"Who do you have to look after you?"

Thin shoulders moved in a halfhearted shrug. The small head turned farther away.

Sweet heaven. With every passing second, Worth felt more and more out of his depth. "Come on, son, help me to help you. Who?" he asked more gently.

The boy sniffed again and tugged his cap lower. "You're a pain, y'know?"

"Evade the question all you like, but you're not getting rid of me until you answer. Who's at home for you?"

"I take care of my gramps, okay?"

He took care. Not the other way around. "And where is your grandfather?" Worth asked, steeling himself against another wave of disquiet. When the youngster reluctantly named the part of town that was his home, he had to swallow the feel of revulsion that rose like bile in his throat.

"Gramps is sick and can't work, so I take care of both of us," the boy declared, as though sensing disapproval.

What kind of work could a young boy do to keep two people fed and a roof over their heads? No wonder he'd grown up to be such a tough little character. What was more, that part of the city was approximately two miles away and began some dangerous territory. Worth guessed anyone living there would have difficulty making it home without a problem; this boy, in his present condition would be pitifully easy prey.

"That does it," Worth muttered, once again taking control of the situation. "You're coming to my place. I'll see you get cleaned up and properly taken care of. We'll worry about the rest later."

"Don't touch me!"

The cry had him smiling wryly, because it struck him as a female protest and proved the boy was operating on sheer bravado. But it didn't keep Worth from scooping the youngster into his arms and carrying him to his car.

He had to take the long way around, because the passenger door was locked; however, it didn't slow him. As he'd initially guessed, the boy was a lightweight. Good Lord, Worth mused, sometimes his briefcase felt heavier.

With more speed than grace, he got his resisting passenger inside the sedan. "Touch that door handle and you'll be sorry," he warned, when the boy scrambled for another means of escape. "I've no intention of hurting you, but I won't let you hobble around these streets, either. You have my word, as soon as we get your leg attended to, I'll drive you anywhere you'd like, all right?"

Worth received no reply. The youngster did, however, cease in his attempt to escape. Shifting as close to the window as he could get, he huddled into a tight ball.

Relieved but weary, Worth shook his head, climbed in behind the wheel and shut the door. Shortly afterward he had the car easing down the road again.

His mind worked much faster.

What was he doing? Was this some latent paternal thing surfacing? Impossible. It certainly wasn't the way he *wanted* to spend Christmas Eve.

At least the kid hadn't pulled a gun or knife.

"Maybe introductions are in order," he said, when the silence became too uncomfortable even for him. "I'm Worth Drury. It's possible that you've seen my name or picture in the paper."

"Don't read the paper."

"Mmm. I have to admit I'm not always thrilled about what's in there myself."

"No, I mean... Forget it."

What had he missed? It had, indeed, been something. "I didn't say that to brag," Worth began again, "but to reassure you."

"Of what?"

"My trustworthiness."

"Right. Like rich people don't commit crimes."

Advantage the runt. Worth reached for the knot of his tie, realized the telling body language, and quickly gripped the steering wheel again. "Okay, so much for reassurances. Why don't you tell me your name?"

His passenger seemed to brood over the matter for a long time. Finally he mumbled with his lowest, most gravelly voice yet, "Rocky."

Nothing could have sounded less suitable. All Worth could think of was the movie character...and the late, real prize fighter. "Ambitious type, are you?"

Except for a brief, scathing look, his passenger didn't respond.

"Er...Rocky what?"

"Jeez. Grimes, okay? What difference does it make?"

At least that part suited him. Thanks to gutter filth, except for a portion of gray knit cap here and a red-and-black patch of coat there, Worth couldn't tell much about what the boy was wearing. Once again he mourned over what this would do to his car's leather seats.

What's more important, Drury, a young life, or a yard or two of cowhide?

Weighed down by his guilt by the time they reached his brownstone, he decided "Rocky" couldn't possibly be more relieved than *he* was. Then the ever-watchful McGuire emerged, somewhat startled, but quick to help him escort their reluctant guest up the stairs and inside.

As expected, his servant didn't attempt to hide his curiosity. Possessing an animated face that stayed in perpetual motion, his slightly bulging but intelligent eyes darted from each successive step, to Rocky, to him, until he obviously came to some private conclusion.

"Is it to be dinner for two after all, sir?"

It was moments like this that had Worth wondering why he kept the man in his employ...other than because McGuire could prepare the most extraordinary feasts with virtually no notice. "Try to keep in mind that I haven't yet given you your Christmas bonus," Worth replied, with a sidelong look of his own. "As for our guest, this is Mr. Rocky Grimes, who briefly aspired to replace my car's hood ornament."

"Ahh..." McGuire's mop of wheat-colored frizz lifted like angel hair in the frigid breeze as he bent to whisper to the boy, "Bad luck, lad. Mr. Drury isn't one for blatant advertisement, no matter what the message. He'll never go for the idea."

When their guest failed to respond, except to grow more rigid between them, Worth cleared his throat and continued with his explanation. "Since he won't let me take him to the hospital, I thought the least we could do is to clean him up before I drive him home."

"Are you saying that's how I'll be spending the rest of the evening, sir? *Christmas Eve.* Cleaning up the lad?"

Looking as though he'd just been drafted by the French Foreign Legion, McGuire closed and bolted the door.

The sound echoed in the quiet but warm house like a dungeon bar being set.

Wide-eyed, Rocky tucked his chin even deeper into the vee of his jacket. But he managed to snarl, "Who asked you to?" and backed into a giant ficus, before hobbling sideways toward the door. "Nobody's touching me. Try and you'll spend the rest of your days singing soprano."

Worth watched McGuire's tawny eyebrows lift and separate like a drawbridge. As bold as the Englishman was himself, it was also clear he hadn't been exposed to too many people like Rocky.

"I've changed my mind," the boy stated, his tone growing tremulous. "I want to leave."

"You wouldn't make it down the stairs without collapsing," Worth told him, noting that in the dim foyer light, the knee looked worse than he'd first thought.

"I *want* to leave. I don't belong here."

"No one's arguing that, but you're here and—" Worth sniffed, again noticing the aroma drifting from Rocky "—we're going to see that we return you in a more presentable state. McGuire, take him up to my bath." He began unbuttoning his coat, for the first time noticed the stains and continued his instructions more wearily, "Help him with whatever he needs. And after he's, er, soaking ... do what you can for his clothes. Or better yet, see what you can find for him to wear, then burn those godawful things."

"Excellent advice, sir. But ..." McGuire scratched delicately at the tip of his nose. "Upstairs? He'll soil the carpets and I only just—"

"Oh, for heaven's sake. I'll do it myself." Frustrated with the whole business, Worth once again lifted the boy into his arms and climbed the stairs. "Do you think you could at least get him something to eat?" he snapped over his shoulder.

His bedroom was at the top of the hall and already lit, since McGuire ritualistically turned on the lights for him every night, as well as turned down the king-size bed. Worth strode into the room and passed the bed without a glance, going straight to the bathroom. There he seated his militant guest on the counter and turned to fill the giant sunken tub. "If you'll strip out of those things, I'll see to your knee. Afterward, I'll find you something to wear. The fit won't thrill you, but at least the quality will be better than those threadbare rags you're wearing."

Satisfied that he had things underway, he faced Rocky again, only to find the boy hadn't budged. He sat as Worth had placed him, his dirty face nearly hidden by his jacket.

"Well? What are you waiting for?"

"Privacy."

He had to be joking! Did the kid think he possessed something anatomically unique?

He matched the boy stare for stare. When it became obvious Rocky wasn't going to relent, Worth uttered a low growl and gave in. "All right. Have it your way. *Again.* But if this is a ploy to hunt around for something to steal—"

"I ain't no thief!"

Poor English aside, there was a strange dignity to the boy's tone and in his bearing, and once again Worth found himself reacting against his nature. With a slow nod, he backed out of the room. "I'll be out here, then. Don't be overly stubborn. If you need anything, yell."

Closing the door behind him, Worth shut his eyes and shook his head. While indescribably relieved that he hadn't seriously injured the boy, he couldn't believe he'd brought him, a complete stranger, into his home. Into the most private part of his house!

Listening for a moment, he satisfied himself that Rocky—what a name, he thought again—had begun moving about. Taking that as a good sign, he went to his armoire and tried to find something that would be appropriate for a squirt his size.

Just as he settled on a black, cable-knit sweater—the darker it was, the less the dirt would show, he told himself—he heard the crash. The scream. A splash.

Expecting the worst, he raced for the bathroom, threw open the door and— He stared incredulously at the horrified young woman sprawled in his bathtub. The *naked,* young woman in his bathtub.

"Oh, my God—" they uttered in unison.

Two
_____

About to duck back under the milky water—on purpose this time—Rocky saw Worth Drury wheel around and present her with his back. As far as she was concerned, it didn't count. Still too upset to be relieved or grateful, she grabbed the first thing she could find, the big sponge she'd knocked into the water when she fell, and flung it at him. "Get out!"

She couldn't have aimed better if she'd tried. The water-soaked missile struck him low, at the base of his head.

"Hey!" Hand to nape, he began to turn, seemed to realize his mistake and quickly swung toward his bedroom again. "That was uncalled for, young lady."

"You're lucky I don't...don't...*ahh-choo!*" The sneeze had her slipping chin-deep, almost as deep as before, into the stinging-hot water. That would teach her, she thought. Nothing like total humiliation, followed by a sneezing fit, to convince her that she shouldn't have helped herself to those pretty crystal things she'd dumped into the tub. Rubbing her itching nose, she glared at Worth Drury's annoyingly broad shoulders. She'd hoped the man would look less intimidating without all of his fancy coats and stuff. He didn't.

"Are you all right?" he asked, his tone cautious.

"Do I *sound* all right?" She snatched at and missed the huge towel she'd set on the bench beside the tub. About to go under again, she clutched at the black marble and fought back an oath of frustration.

"I suppose," he drawled, "you won't be happy until there's as much water *outside* the tub as *inside?*"

"Go stuff yourself."

He sighed. "Let's try again, shall we? Is there anything I can do or get for you?"

"Don't you think you've done enough for one night?"

"Now look here, none of this would have happened if—" He bit back whatever else he'd been about to say and gripped the doorknob. "Why didn't you tell me you were a girl?"

His hands were strong, but elegant. She didn't have to look at her own to know that he would find them an embarrassment in comparison. Not that she cared, of course. She worked hard, hard enough for two people. She didn't have time to pamper herself like some people did. "For the same reason I don't run around in a ball gown and high heels," she shot back, forcing herself to ignore the powerful figure he cut and glare at his partially drenched dark brown hair. Did the man think she had no sense of—what did you call it?—self-preservation? He had to know it was safer traveling through the streets at night looking like a poor street kid than her own sex. "And for your information I'm a *woman,* not a girl."

"You've a vivid imagination, too."

Rocky almost missed the dry response, but not quite. Unfortunately, by the time she caught on, he'd drawn the door closed behind himself. Creep, she thought, finally allowing herself to lower her guard and let her body catch up with the last hour's events.

She moaned softly. There wasn't an inch of her that didn't hurt. So bad that she didn't want to look, let alone touch. But she did both—because of Mr. Almighty Drury's parting shot. A person didn't need a degree to figure out *that* had been a slam.

What was so wrong with her figure? she wondered, forcing herself to sit up so she could inspect what showed above the water line. Okay, maybe she wasn't Miss Centerfold of the Year, but for her size she had enough of what she needed to qualify as Species Past Puberty. The jerk. What did he know about real women, anyway, living in this...museum.

Resentful, she eyed the room once again. Like the rest of the house it was gorgeous...huge...ritzy. Did that make him a prince? He'd practically turned her into a stain on the road. It would serve him right if she made him pay for the fright he'd given her. Only, she wasn't a person to do that. All she wanted, *needed* to do was to get home. That's why she'd been racing in the first place.

Reminded of what was hard to forget at the best of times, she snatched up the washcloth that matched the burgundy bath towel, wet and soaped it, and began scrubbing at her face. The faster she got this over with, the sooner she could get Badger his stuff.

A girl. Worth tried to assimilate the information into his mind but found it difficult. It had been bad enough thinking he'd almost killed a kid, but then to have walked in on a girl in his bathroom...

"I'm a woman."

There was no denying that.

He should be feeling relieved, considering the mess—no, the threat he could've faced if she'd really been a minor. The mere thought of the authorities being called in, the lawyers, the press...it was enough to make him break out in a cold sweat. As it was, he only needed to adjust to the shock...his shame at having spoken, reacted as he had...and deal with a sudden, gut-deep surge of self-preservation. Strangely enough, that impulse was almost as strong as the others. Maybe because it was his most masculine instinct, he understood the latter most of all. Why? Because without all that filth and the camouflage of her rags "Rocky" Grimes was a beauty.

His heart had stopped the instant he'd seen her. Granted, she'd been sprawled half in and out of the tub and had looked half-drowned; however, with her pale, firm breasts heaving as she'd tried to catch her breath, her slender shoulders and surprisingly long legs, she'd left him speechless. Perhaps she was too thin for classical beauty and, granted, the tangle of hair tumbling wildly down her back and fanning out in the water needed more than one scrubbing to bring out its raven black luster—nevertheless, he hadn't been so stunned by anything since...

Good Lord, he must be mad. He'd been about to equate her with his *Galatea*.

Ridiculous. Worth crossed over to the armoire and retrieved the sweater. Unbidden, the image of Rocky raising her arms and drawing the soft wool over her bare, sleek curves flashed before his mind's eye. The pose came so close to matching that of his statue's there was no stopping the sexual hunger that stirred deep inside him.

Damn it, she's a kid, practically young enough to be your daughter. What kind of despicable worm are you?

He had to have been wrong. It must have been the play of light, her pose, the fact that he'd been thinking about Galatea earlier that had triggered the comparison. He'd just been caught off guard, that's all. The similarities were superficial.

"Where would you like this, sir?"

Embarrassed, he turned and saw McGuire in the doorway bearing a silver tray. Worth made a small ceremony of glancing around, finally gesturing toward the table nearest the bathroom door. As he watched his employee cross the room, an idea struck him.

"McGuire, you wear jeans, don't you?"

The shorter man snapped to attention. "Only during my time off. I swear it!"

"I don't care about when, only that you do. I need a pair."

"You, sir?"

"They'll undoubtedly still be too large for her, but you're considerably smaller than me. Will you donate them?" When the man continued to gape, Worth scowled. "For pity's sake. Naturally, I intend to reimburse you!"

"It's not that, Mr. Drury. It's...did you say 'her'?" His eyes resembled a beached fish as he shifted his gaze to the bathroom door. "You mean the bloke's of the female persuasion?"

"You're many things, McGuire, not all of them commendable. But the one thing you aren't is deaf."

"Oh, well, that's very kind of you, sir." His pleased expression turned to one of curiosity. "Er, may I ask then, how you discovered our guest's, um ... ?"

"You may not. Just get the pants, would you? Please," he added, pained over what this episode was doing to his self-control.

As soon as McGuire was gone, Worth rubbed his forehead. He wished he could afford to pour himself a drink. Unfortunately, he had to drive Rock—Miss Grimes, he amended silently, home shortly. He didn't need to take any chances.

McGuire returned in impressive haste. Worth took both the jeans and the sweater and approached the bathroom door. He knocked softly. "Hello?"

"Don't you come in here!"

"She's certainly a feisty one, isn't she?" McGuire said, at his shoulder.

"Do you mind?" Worth shot him a glare. "I think I can handle things from here."

"You might want a witness."

"For *what?*"

"In case the sneaky...er, young lady accuses you of something. Why just this week there was a story about such a thing in the *National Reporter.*"

"McGuire," Worth growled, wondering if his day could get any worse. "Spare me."

"Yes, sir. Will there be anything else? Socks? Undies? I could—"

"Get out."

"Immediately. I'll be in the kitchen if you should require anything."

"That ice in my study when I return from driving *Miss Grimes* home."

When McGuire backed out of the room, albeit with a suspicious twitch working around his mobile mouth, Worth glanced down at the clothes he held and then at the bathroom door again. Like it or not, there was no other way to get them to her without opening it.

He knocked again.

"Go away!"

"I need to slip your clothes inside."

"Touch that knob and I'll scream the place down."

The possibility that someone next door or outside might hear her and phone for the police deserved consideration. But so did having to look at her again in her filthy, torn clothing. That made up Worth's mind for him.

"Yell all you want," he called back, "but I'm handing them inside."

Careful to keep his face averted, he pushed the door open, just enough to shove in the jeans and sweater. He fully expected another wallop on the head for his troubles, but it didn't happen.

Grateful, if curious, he lifted his gaze to the vanity mirror and saw her huddling behind a bath towel that covered everything the marble didn't. Everything but her midnight blue eyes. It made her look like something between a novitiate and an houri.

Disturbed by the idea, Worth withdrew and shut the door.

"McGuire's brought up a tray for you," he called. "Don't linger too long or the food will get cold."

She didn't reply.

For the next few minutes, he paced the length of the bedroom, listening to every sound coming from inside the bathroom, wondering what he should say when she came out. Being at a loss for words wasn't a trait he suffered from, but then no one like Rocky Grimes had ever crashed into his life before, either. Lord, what a name. What a mess!

It seemed like an eternity, but finally, just when he'd been about to knock on the door again, it opened. He stared, unable to help himself from doing otherwise.

She emerged wearing the things he'd provided. Her own clothes were bundled into her coat, which she'd turned inside out and had tied into a knot. She held the bulky mass close, as though they were the crown jewels. But what had him staring was the woman herself.

Black hair like a silk mantle reached her waist and glistened with the same indigo lights that shimmered in her eyes. The skin he'd thought as merely pale was actually translucent, the same way collectors described the finest porcelain. Features that had seemed just youthful at first, he now recognized as delicate—a straight nose, high cheekbones, a petal-sculpted mouth.... She made him think of a gamine gypsy, a woods nymph. No, he realized as she approached him hesitantly, there was no avoiding the obvious. She did resemble *Galatea*.

"I thought I'd put my shoes on downstairs," she murmured, indicating the scuffed-up sneakers tucked beneath the bundle.

Worth's gaze fell to dainty toes peering out from beneath the too-long jeans. "No problem." His tongue felt too heavy for his mouth. He sucked in a new, rejuvinating breath. "Why don't you set those things down and have something to eat?"

Although she cast a yearning glance toward the tray, which even he had to admit was giving off luscious aromas, she shook her head. "I have to go."

"You can't leave with your hair soaking wet. You'll catch your death out there. That forecasted front's arriving and the temperature's dropping. We could have snow before you got home."

She dug something from a back pocket. "I'll put on my hat."

The cap wasn't as filthy as the rest of her clothes, but Worth grimaced at the thought of the rough, dull wool hiding what had turned out to be a vast improvement in her appearance. "A few spoonfuls of soup and a bite of the sandwich isn't going to—"

"Look," she said, tense and nervous, "I have to deliver something, okay?"

The tighter she clutched her bundle, the more suspicious Worth became. Had she stolen something after all? He didn't think there was anything of real value lying around in the bathroom, unless... Maybe he'd forgotten a ring or tie clip?

As the possibility grew more firm in his mind, he could feel the muscles around his mouth tensing. "What are you hiding?"

"Nothing."

She *had* been tempted. Disappointment hardened in him. "Put it back. Do it now, and I won't say a word."

"You're crazy," she scoffed, and started for the door. "I don't have anything that's yours, except this stuff you gave me to wear."

"Oh, no, you don't." Worth grabbed her arm. The shoes fell out of her grasp, but she kept a tight hold on the bundle. "Let go, young lady, or you'll have to explain your actions to someone less sympathetic than I am."

"This is mine and none of your business!"

"Anyone and anything in this house is my business." With a brutal jerk, he pulled the parcel from her hands and, tight-lipped, shook it loose. Clothes tumbled to the floor and then a small vial.

Revulsion turned him rigid. "So you're even worse than a liar."

"No!" She lunged to pick it up.

Worth was faster. Snatching it into his hand, he held the bottle high over his head and out of her reach. "I will not have drugs in my house."

"Give it back, you..." She hopped up, trying to reach it, then shoved at his chest. "I *need* it, mister."

"I can imagine. There's nothing more pitiful than a junkie."

"I'm no junkie!"

Impassioned, she proved even more captivating, and beyond his anger, Worth was struck with the sadness of the situation. That was the way of it these days, he thought. Kids were growing up looking for the easy way out. Well, he would make sure this one didn't succeed.

"Behave," he told her, "and be grateful I'm not already on the phone with the authorities."

"Go ahead and do it. Only you're the one who's gonna look like a fool."

"Don't push your luck, Miss Grimes. I'm trying to remember that it is Christmas Eve and—"

"It's insulin, you big jerk!"

He froze. Dazed, he glanced down at his hand. For the first time he took a moment to inspect the bottle more closely, turn it around and read the label. When he saw she'd been telling the truth, he didn't know whether he felt more embarrassed or relieved. Then came another, more poignant emotion—lately a rare one for him. Compassion.

"You're diabetic?"

"No. Badger is."

"Who's Badger?"

"My grandfather," she snapped, and thrust out her hand. "Now give that to me. I gotta get home and give him his shot. He can't take good care of himself like I can, and I know he's been without a shot for longer than it's safe."

Worth looked from her fierce, blue eyes to her trembling hand and made his decision. He handed back her property. "I'll drive you."

"I told you, my neighborhood—"

"Is delightful," Worth said, finishing for her as she rebundled her things. "I appreciate the reminder. I'm sure tonight will go down in the annals of my life's history as one of the most enlightening, if not entertaining. Now move. And grab that sandwich while you're at it. No sense for it to go to waste."

Within minutes he had her back in his car and was asking for directions. She gave them resentfully. It reminded him of what a hard time he'd put her through tonight, first by almost killing her, then mortifying her when he'd walked in on her in an indelicate moment and finally accusing her of being one of life's failures. What else could he do wrong?

"I know it doesn't begin to make up for tonight, but I'm sorry," he murmured, when it became clear she didn't intend to speak to him again.

She drew a deep breath as though to reply, only to turn her head away and look out the passenger window. Worth refocused on the street, telling himself he should leave well enough alone.

As predicted, snow began to fall. At least those who believed in Santa Claus and magic would be pleased. He hadn't believed in either for years and wondered if his passenger ever had.

"How do you manage?" he asked, when curiosity got the best of him. "Insulin isn't cheap. What do you do for a living?"

"I don't turn tricks, if that's what you're thinking."

Since few people ever dared speak to him this way—even Chase and McGuire knew there were boundaries they couldn't cross—it was impossible to repress his annoyance completely. "Thank you for restoring my faith in male intelligence," he shot back. "Dressed as you were, it would hardly have proved a profitable venture."

"You're one laugh after another, aren't you?"

As quickly as it had come, his ire cooled. "Excuse me. Sometimes I overindulge my affinity for the sardonic."

"Yeah, and you talk weird, too."

Although he kept his eyes on the road, Worth couldn't help arching an eyebrow. "I beg your pardon, but I'll have you know that I was president of my college debating team."

His passenger uttered another disparaging sound. "Badger'd tell you all those high-dollar words ain't worth nothing on the streets."

"Ah, well, who am I to disagree with the Plato of the Bowery?"

"Who?"

Startled that she hadn't at least a rudimentary awareness of the philosopher, he asked, "Just how old are you, anyway?"

She sat up straighter. "What's that got to do with anything?"

"Humor me."

"I'm twenty."

Older than she looked. Definitely older than her education would seem to suggest. While that made him feel slightly better for having had the physical reaction to her that he did, he wondered about the pressures and limitations the age put on her life, her future.

"How old are you?"

"Thirty-six," he murmured, more interested in her. "So, er, what *do* you do? For a living, I mean."

This time she didn't go immediately hostile. "Lots of things," she replied with a shrug. "Whatever will earn me a few bucks. I don't hold only one job, though. Can't find any that pays enough to support us."

"Us meaning you and Ba—your grandfather?"

"Yeah."

"Is he too ill to work?"

It took a moment for her to answer, but she finally murmured, "He probably could, except . . . he drinks."

Uncomfortably aware of how shallow any words of sympathy would sound, Worth said nothing. They came to an intersection, and he requested further directions. After making the turn she'd indicated, he asked, "Where did you work today?"

"I washed dishes at a restaurant."

"Sounds like grueling work."

"Then I ran some errands for a bookie. . . ."

The disconcerting news had Worth shooting her a doubtful look. "You're kidding?"

She moved one shoulder in an indifferent shrug. "It pays best, and as far as I'm concerned, I'm only picking up and delivering envelopes."

"Still, it could be dangerous."

"So's crossing the street," she replied with considerable aplomb. "Anyway, I finished the day at a clinic, where they pay me to clean up. That's how I get Badger's medicine. One of the doctors there knows about him."

"My God. You must be exhausted."

"Well, my feet were kinda sore, but compared to what the rest of me feels like right now, I guess they're not so bad."

Her story made Worth ashamed. He had no business feeling sorry for himself when people like her risked so much just to make ends meet. In fact, she made him feel like one of Dickens's villains.

Casting another glance her way, he noticed her look hungrily at the carefully held sandwich she'd wrapped in the napkin McGuire had provided. He said, "Why don't you eat that before it turns to stone?"

"I thought I'd share it with Badger. Turn by that red-and-blue sign."

Worth followed her instructions, but his thoughts were on what she'd said. Did that mean the sandwich would be their only meal tonight? He hadn't thought she could make him feel worse, but she'd just succeeded.

They drove another minute or so in silence and then she said, "Stop."

This couldn't be it, he thought with a sinking feeling. Despite what she'd implied, and even with the added beauty of huge snowflakes falling around the car, the run-down block of buildings she'd had him stop by filled him with a new dread. And that alley she was peering down didn't help.

"If you could wait a second, I'll change and bring out your stuff."

Her unease was palpable. "That's not necessary," he said, equally unhappy with the idea of her going down there alone. "Keep it." Then he glanced past her again. "Which apartment's yours?"

"It's, um, not really an apartment."

"I don't understand. Do you or don't you live here?"

"What's it to you, anyway? I live down there, all right? Curiosity satisfied?"

She pointed to where a dim glow emanated from a mud-splattered, grilled basement window. Worth found the lump that formed in his throat a blessing. It kept him from blurting out that it wasn't all right with him. No, he thought, not at all; however, neither was it any of his business.

Nevertheless, he felt obligated to do something more.

Shifting, he reached into his coat for his billfold and without bothering to identify the bills, pulled out several. But when he began to pass them to her, she pushed away his hand as though it was a weapon.

"What do you think you're doing?" she demanded.

"Trying to help."

"I don't take charity." She threw open her door and scrambled out.

"Wait! Take it," he urged. "It's nothing, really."

As soon as he said it, he knew he'd made a mistake. A terrible look came over her face.

"It is to me."

She slammed the door and ran.

Rocky raced through the darkness, for once not cautious about what might be lurking behind a Dumpster or a packing crate. She had to fight back tears of anger and fatigue.

Tonight wasn't going at all the way she'd planned. Despite the expense of Badger's medicine, she'd managed to put a little money aside in the hopes of buying a few special treats for the holidays. But she hadn't bought anything yet, and the way she was feeling . . . At this point she would be lucky to get to church for the candlelight service, let alone the market. That's the only reason she'd accepted the sandwich from Worth Drury.

Worth Drury. As she fought her protesting joints and muscles, she hurried down the basement stairs to get away from the cold and the man she was silently calling several choice names she hadn't already thought of.

All this was his fault. He'd made her so late she was almost sick with worry about Badger. Not that she didn't always worry about him. But the longer she stayed away from home, the more she feared Gramps had managed to scrounge up enough change for a cheap bottle of wine. Christmas always proved the toughest time for his demons. What if someone down at the corner bar had, in the spirit of the holidays, bought him a few rounds?

That's why she'd been racing so and why she'd gotten careless crossing the street. The only reason she'd made herself later was because she'd been so embarrassed with the way she'd looked and smelled.

She supposed she should be grateful to the man for not just leaving her in the gutter. It was hard, though. He didn't have the most winning nature.

But he was an amazing-looking man. What those male fashion magazines would call elegant, she thought, as she fumbled for her key. Sophisticated. Too stiff for her tastes, though. When he'd attempted a smile, she'd thought his strong-molded features would crack. And there was something cold about him, as well. It made his metal gray eyes seem all the more ruthless. She'd had to really psyche herself out not to lose her courage around him.

Even so, when he'd carried her upstairs, there had been something; the feel of hard muscles, the strong beat of his heart... maybe it was the mellow hint of his after-shave, who knows. At any rate, he'd made her wonder for a second, wonder about womanly things—a first for her—which had made it all the more embarrassing when she'd lost her balance and he'd walked in on her in the bathroom.

Cripes. She'd wanted to die.

Well, it was over. She could put it behind her, because sure as she believed that trouble came in groups of three, she knew she wouldn't be seeing Mr. Worth Drury again.

Rocky shivered. Even in the pit of the basement's stairwell, the heavy snowflakes pricked her skin, they were so cold. But the wind was worse. It felt as though she wasn't wearing her cap and made her painfully aware of her wet hair.

Finally locating her key, she shoved it into the dead bolt that she'd installed herself. Sneezing, she hurried inside, not wanting to think about the coat she would have liked to have bought with the money.

"Badger—I'm home!" Slamming the door behind her, she quickly set the lock. The relief she always felt when she made it through the alley without incident was as warming as that fireplace fire she'd glimpsed at Worth Drury's. Rocky frowned and slid the secondary lock into place. It wouldn't do to remember too much; it would just remind her of all they didn't have here.

Except for the small night-light in what they called the kitchenette, their one-room home was dark. She was used to that, though. Even in pitch blackness she could have found the only other lamp they owned. She'd rescued the orange-and-black fixture from one of the trash Dumpsters in the alley. Badger said it was the ugliest thing he'd ever seen and would rather live in the dark instead of turning it on—which he often did. Rocky considered herself more pragmatic. Man, she liked that word. Dr. Greenway had called her that when they'd first met, and she'd had to ask him what it meant. It made her feel strong, and sometimes when life seemed to work overtime to stack the odds against her, she needed all the help she could get. As for the lamp, it worked, and it had been free. That's all that mattered.

When the light snapped on, she turned and spotted Badger in his usual place, lying on the threadbare recliner he often slept in throughout the night. Rocky smiled, relieved that she wouldn't have to go to the streets and hunt for him.

"Wake up, sleepyhead. It's time to take your shot and get ready for church. I promised Father Carmichael I'd play Mary for the living Nativity scene this year, remember?"

The thought of having to kneel for Father C's entire sermon made her want to groan. Jeez, she thought, her knee. Then she thought of who she was playing tonight and shame filled her. What was a little bump compared to what Mary had endured?

"You won't believe what happened to me this evening," she continued, determined to sound more cheerful as she set her bundle on the floor outside the bathroom. She placed the sandwich on the kitchen table. "I got hit by a car. Don't worry though, 'cause I'm okay. But it was kinda spooky for a minute, you know? Badger... ?"

Gosh, she thought, he was sure sleeping deep tonight.

Suddenly uneasy, Rocky crossed to him. "Gramps?"

What? she thought, her fear growing. What was wrong? Had his sugar count gone haywire? Had he slipped into what she'd feared most—a coma?

Reaching his side, she dropped to the cement floor and forced herself to bite back the cry of pain when she hit her injured knee. Anxious, she touched Badger's lips, fumbled for his hand, felt for his pulse.

Denial came like a blast of frigid wind. The tears she'd successfully held back from Worth Drury now rushed free, as though a spillway had finally been pried open.

Rocky collapsed against his unmoving chest. "Oh, God... Gramps! *Grampa!*"

Three

"And you're going to fall off that pew from exhaustion, if you don't go home and get some rest, child."

Rocky jerked upright, blinked and looked up into the kind, ruddy face of Father Carmichael. "Sorry, Father. Did you need something?" Hearing how her voice carried in the cathedral, Rocky added in a loud whisper, "Is it Mrs. Mulvaney? I told her that cold needed to run its course. Tell her to go on to bed. I can chaperone the kids while they're having their party."

"No need, no need. Dani was able to finish with her business, after all, and she's volunteered to stay at the hostel and take Mrs. Mulvaney's place. What I need *you* to do is not run yourself into the ground," the priest replied, laying a calming hand on her shoulder. "Rocky, listen to yourself. You're going ninety miles an hour trying so hard to run away from your problems. When will you accept that Badger's passing wasn't your fault? His poor body gave out, that's all. Now you have to get on with your life."

"*He* was my life, Father C," she said to the elderly priest, who looked more like a steelworker than a shepherd of men. "He was all the family I had in the world, you know that."

With a sigh, the silver-haired man with the marine haircut eased his stout frame down onto the polished but aging pew. "Yes, and you cared for him with a devotion that was inspiring. But that role is done, child. It's time to move on to other tasks and adventures lying before you."

Rocky tossed her head in a brief, silent laugh. "Adventures. Oh, sure. The world won't keep turning if I don't wash my share of dishes and scrub my share of bathrooms. Fat Louie would have to give up the bookie business if he didn't have me to run for him."

Father Carmichael winced. "Rocky, you *know* you're not supposed to tell me about that."

"C'mon, Father. Your boss lets you reap in megabucks on bingo. Big difference."

"We've been through that before, and you know the difference between fund-raising and gambling for profit."

Although the priest spoke gently, Rocky bit her lip. "I'm sorry. I don't mean to be so awful."

"Grief comes out of everyone in its own way," he replied, patting her tightly clasped hands. "But it's been a week now, and I'm worrying about your inability to rise out of your depression, Rocky. Even the youngsters at the hostel are beginning to notice you're withdrawing more."

With a gasp, Rocky cried, "How can they say that? I've been keeping to the schedule I've always had. I'm there for them every day I can be!"

Father Carmichael stilled her. "Listen to me. It's not about *being* somewhere. Like Dani, you're the kind of person who has more to give than many other people do."

Being compared to someone she held in near reverence, whom most of the community saw, not as a social worker but a godsend, would have thrilled Rocky at any other time. At the moment, though, it was a weight she couldn't bear and a compliment she didn't deserve.

"Yes, you are," her priest and friend insisted. "Only that great wealth of energy, that gift you were given can only flow when it's given freely. Do you understand?"

"I'm not sure I do."

Father Carmichael smiled and shook his head. "I can see you don't. If only I had more lambs in my flock who were as guileless as you. What I'm trying to say is that you're a powerhouse when you're doing something from the heart, Rocky. But right now your heart is like a sieve and there's no reservoir from which to share with others."

Rocky bowed her head. "I've been selfish."

"No, child. I'm suggesting that perhaps a good way to redirect all that turmoil inside you would be to share it with those who understand your pain and those who need the lessons you're learning from it."

"But...I don't know if I am learning anything, Father. No, that's not true, either." She chewed on her lower lip, wondering if she dared say what she'd begun to feel. "I'm beginning to doubt there's any hope, Father C. Nothing really changes for us in this part of town, especially for the kids like me who are dropouts or those who are orphans or whatever. We can't get decent jobs that would get us ahead because we don't have an education, and we don't have an education because we have to work at low-paying jobs to survive. The system's against us."

The priest nodded, his expression somber. "Everything you say is true, and it was our Lord Himself who said that the poor will always be with us. But that doesn't mean we should give up in our attempt to improve our lives. You know what the Good Book also says about help coming to those who help themselves?"

He had a point there. At least she accepted that nothing could get better if she was wallowing in self-pity. But Father Carmichael was wrong about how sharing her misery could be helpful to someone else. The way she saw it, that only created a chorus of whiners.

No, the answer lay in her old theory about money being the answer to the problem. She had to have more, bunches, before she would feel she was really in a position to help anyone. And maybe if she succeeded ... maybe she could forgive herself for having failed her gramps.

"I'll work on it, Father," she said, trying to give him a reassuring smile.

"Good girl. Now why don't we go join the New Year's party? When I left, Dani had about coaxed Eddie into showing the girls a few of the self-defense moves he's been learning at those martial arts classes she arranged for him."

"If you don't mind, I'm not quite ready for celebrations. But Happy New Year, Father." She stood and kissed his sandpapery rough cheek.

"Happy New Year, dear Rocky. Be careful going home."

Minutes later she crossed the last intersection to her block. Traffic was almost nonexistent, now that most people were already either home from work or at a party. The bitter cold was keeping pedestrians off the sidewalks, as well. Every once in a while she could hear the sound of music and laughter coming from an apartment. The cheerful sounds made her feel less alone, and the extra lights that spilled onto the street quieted some of her fear. But she would have been naive if she'd believed that she was really any safer than usual. It was bad enough that she actually looked more like a female tonight, since she wasn't wearing a hat that hid her hair.

Don't focus on trouble, she told herself, and tried to concentrate on happier thoughts. She recalled last New Year's Eve when she and Badger had both gone to the hostel's party. It had been one of Badger's better periods. He'd entertained everyone with stories about his days on a tugboat and had played his harmonica until the morning hours.

God, she missed him. Crazy old coot. She hoped he appreciated that she'd spent every extra dollar she'd hoarded away for a down payment on a decent apartment for them, to pay for a nice coffin for him. Most important, though, she wished he knew how awful it was to go back to that dark pit of an apartment, knowing he wouldn't be there to smile, complain or tell her the newest joke he'd heard on the streets.

As she approached the alley, a muffled noise made her stop. What was that? she wondered, immediately tense. A cat? Probably one of their atomic-sized rats. Or was it a two-legged variety of rodent? Damn, she brooded, clenching her hands in her pockets. She didn't want to walk down that dark alley alone.

"Hey, Rocky."

She spun around, fear replacing her surprise. That slick, insolent voice belonged to only one person, the most arrogant thug in this neighborhood. She dreaded even the sight of his souped-up car cruising the streets, and although he often made suggestive comments to her, she'd never believed he'd been actually serious. Why should he be, when he always had two or three girls following him around like shadows? But tonight he stood alone, silhouetted against a streetlight.

"What do you want, Speed?" she demanded, struggling to keep her nervousness out of her voice. Not much over average height, he made up in strength what he lacked in size. Even in the imperfect lighting, she could see his hooded eyes gauging and deciding.

"Is that any way to talk to somebody who's come to extend his condolences?"

He was as slick as he was dark, and Rocky didn't trust him any more than she believed she could win a physical fight with him. That made her all the more determined to find out what he wanted. What didn't reassure her was hearing that he knew about her grandfather. Of course, it made sense that he *would* know. Nothing happened on these streets without Speed finding out about it. But that meant he also knew she was living alone now, that she had no one to turn to for even the slightest protection.

"You're a little late," she said, lifting her chin.

"Well, you know I like to choose my own ground, and it ain't that church you hang out at. I thought maybe you and me, we could keep each other company," he continued, taking a step closer. "This being a party night and all. You feel like partying, sweet thing?"

Rocky swallowed against the dryness of her mouth and throat. "No. And whatever it is that you're selling, I'm not interested."

"Show some respect, Mama," another voice crooned from behind her in the alley. "My man Speed don't have to be polite, especially to some half-pint chicky with an attitude."

Trapped. With fear swelling into outright terror, Rocky spun around. It made her hair whip across her eyes, and she frantically raked it out of the way. Suddenly she knew she'd been foolish to hope; there was nothing accidental or even social about this meeting. Speed had come for her.

Free again—at least for a few hours. Worth drove through the snow-lined streets feeling more relieved the farther he distanced himself from his father's house. W.H.'s party had been beyond tedious, it had been depressing. False sincerity, excessive self-interest...and that redundant lecture from the old tyrant about the necessity for marrying and marrying well.... It had been too much, and Chase hadn't helped with that unsubtle innuendo about how he might still be pining for Erica.

The problem, although Worth hadn't wasted his time trying to explain it to either member of his family, had everything to do with boredom and nothing to do with the heart or fickleness. Rather than say something he might later regret, however, he'd chosen the wisest alternative and had left.

What did either of them know about how he felt or what he needed? He wasn't certain whether he did himself. Not completely. He only knew he wanted a change, something new in his life, a mountain worthy of climbing, a challenge big enough to test him. His work still interested him, but all the socializing and the politics that went with it...what a bore.

At the next light he turned left. A strange tingling sensation danced through him, and he didn't have to think hard to realize what brought it on. This was where he'd met Rocky Grimes.

Now *there* was someone he doubted ever had to worry about boredom the way he did. At least thinking about her situation got him away from brooding about his life.

Was she all right?

Was she safe?

Does she ever think about me?

Good grief, where had that come from? She was barely more than a kid. Telling himself he was being a fool, he accelerated past the site, but it didn't stop him from remembering.

Rocky Grimes was no kid. Throughout the week, no matter how much he'd tried to ignore it, the scene in his bathroom flashed before his eyes. With it had come a phantom restlessness unlike his other restlessness as well as a yearning he didn't feel comfortable with, either.

Ridiculous, he fumed, as it rose again. He had no business focusing on that episode or on her. She was a street kid. He was born with the proverbial silver spoon in his mouth. They were more than complete opposites, they might as well be from different planets.

But was she all right?

When he found himself turning away from his own neighborhood, he realized he needed to find out.

"I don't believe you're doing this."

He couldn't believe he was talking to himself.

He told himself to look at the bright side; chances were he wouldn't find her street again, let alone her building. If he did manage, then what? Did he expect her to be standing out on the sidewalk waiting for him? He couldn't very well go up to her door and knock. For what?

No, he wouldn't find it.

He found it.

"Great. Now you can rent yourself out as a homing pigeon," he growled to himself, just as his headlights picked up several figures near her alley. He wasn't into block parties.

But that wasn't a party going on. As he drew closer, he saw there were only three people, and they were scuffling.

It was none of his business. Right off the top of his head he could think of a dozen reasons to floor the gas pedal and get the hell away from there. Then his headlights picked out that the smaller figure between the two taller ones had long black hair, and suddenly his body shifted into some kind of automatic pilot mode.

Worth slammed on the brakes, and the car screeched to a halt. As he jumped out, he had no idea whether or not it would continue rolling down the street. All he could see was that she was putting up the fight of her life.

He charged, forgetting or ignoring that he'd lived thirty-six years without ever having used his fists. Rocky's scream of terror obliterated the privilege of acknowledging that.

Blinded by an emotion that had no name, he attacked, grabbing, swinging and delivering blows that shook his entire body. No longer a thinking entity, he used his size and power to control the moment. When a fist clipped his mouth, he only felt it on some second or third level. His own fists would not be stopped. Even when he heard a curse and the order, "Let's get outta here," he raged on. It took spinning around, finding himself without an opponent and face-to-face with Rocky to make him freeze in mid-punch.

Worth glanced around in time to see her attackers disappear around the corner. Seconds later his brain reinterpreted pain for his body. Sabers diced at his fingers, a rubber mallet bounced off his mouth, and cathedral bells clamored in his head.

Acutely aware that people like him didn't do things like this, he gasped for breath and managed to ask, "Are you . . . all right?"

"Yeah, but you're not." She tore off a glove and came to him, reached up and touched his mouth. Worth wondered which of them looked more amazed, when she held up fingers stained with his blood.

"Wait a second," she mumbled, and dug into her coat pockets. "I have some tissues."

It was the same coat she'd been wearing when he knocked her into the gutter. "That's okay," he began— and gasped. The mallet grew claws. Having no great desire to experience the feeling again, he reached inside his coat and tuxedo jacket and drew out a handkerchief.

Rocky gaped at the immaculate linen. "You can't use that. The blood'll stain it."

Worth decided one square of cloth didn't warrant that much concern. Touching the handkerchief to his mouth, he discovered his lower lip was already swelling to an abnormal size. His immediate thought was of gratitude; he was glad he didn't have to be anywhere tomorrow.

"So, what're you doing here?"

He could imagine her question being echoed by an assortment of people, ranging from emergency room attendants, to McGuire, to his insurance agent. But he doubted any of them would look at him with such wariness. Worth shrugged, trying to avoid having to move his lip.

Rocky narrowed her eyes. "Just out for an evening ride, huh?"

"Something like that," he managed with difficulty.

"Not too smart."

"Look who's talking."

As he grunted against another spasm of pain, she hung her head. Up until then she'd been the Rocky Grimes he'd remembered—a bit shaky because of the scare she'd experienced, but still cocky, still fighting. Now, abruptly, he saw the fight drain out of her. She wrapped her arms around herself, and what Worth could see of her pale face turned as white as the partial moon peering through her alley. It made her seem all the more vulnerable.

He forgot about his injuries. He forgot the condition of her coat, too. Instead, following an impulse much stronger than any external thing, he stepped forward and put his arms around her. "It's over. Focus on that."

She exhaled, the sound like a breeze stirring autumn leaves. "I've never been so scared." Her body shook just as much.

Worth felt her clutch handfuls of the back of his coat and hang on. It made him feel very capable, solid, and he tightened his arms. "It's okay."

"They were gonna..."

He lowered his chin to the top of her head. She fit there. Some of the power returned. "But they didn't. They're gone now."

"Because of you."

It wasn't a legitimate thank-you, but Worth almost smiled—or at least he would have, if his lips could have formed one. Instead, he stroked her back and her hair. Contentment replaced his relief and fury, and warmed him. How soft, he thought, how incredibly soft the silky mass was. An elusive scent rose from it, too, flirting with his senses. The image of meadows filled his mind... meadows in the moonlight.

Perhaps he'd suffered a concussion.

"Let me park my car," he said, struggling for some logic. "I'll walk you inside and help you explain things to your grandfather."

A shudder ran through her body.

"What is it? What's wrong?"

She didn't answer at first. He soon realized it wasn't because she was ignoring him, she was fighting tears. He'd never been able to bear being around a crying woman. Not that he didn't know how to act when they did weep; but too often tears were used as weapons. Was that what he was dealing with here?

All his instincts rejected the idea. He had a feeling that the only reason tough, young Rocky Grimes was tearing up was because she couldn't *not* cry.

"Talk to me," he whispered at last.

"He's dead."

Worth didn't have to ask for a clarification. The night grew darker and huge, and the trembling woman in his arms felt infinitely more fragile. He took a moment to alter his stance, like a pilot trying to keep his balance as he navigated a boat through turbulent waters.

Stabilized, he glanced around, particularly down the alley. Had he missed seeing the old man's body? No, he couldn't have. After those two hoods ran, Rocky would have raced to her grandfather—if the old man had been around here. That meant only one thing.

"When?" he asked, knowing there was no other response he could make.

It seemed to take her forever for her to answer. "The night we...you...I came home and he was gone."

While he'd been bullying her and thinking—no, he wouldn't dwell on what he'd been thinking. But Worth swore under his breath. He also made a decision.

"Come on."

"Where?"

He indicated his car and began leading her to it. "You're shaking from more than shock, you're frozen through and through. You need to sit down."

"But I live right here."

Worth glanced over his shoulder. Tonight there wasn't even a hint of a light coming through the basement window. He didn't want to think about how dark, cold and damp it was in there.

"Do you really want to be there tonight? Alone?"

She didn't meet his probing gaze, but she did shake her head.

"And those two thugs," Worth continued, "what if they came back? What if they know where you live?"

"They do."

"That settles it, then."

Before either of them spoke again, Worth had her in the car and was heading for the next intersection.

"Why are you doing this?" Rocky asked him, breaking that silence.

"I don't know." It was as truthful as he could be without doing any intense examinations.

It seemed acceptable to her. "Where are we going?"

"Home. To my home."

"Is that a polite way of telling me I need another bath?"

Worth knew then that she was beginning to recover. He relaxed somewhat. "If that's what you want."

"The question is, what do you want?" She used her sleeve to finish wiping dry her face. "I may not have your years of experience, but that doesn't mean I believe in fairy tales."

"Should I be relieved or disappointed?"

"What I mean is that people like you don't usually go out of your way to get personally involved with people like me. Your kind finds that your checkbook keeps you from getting your hands dirty."

"Is that what you'd prefer? Money?"

"Maybe you'd better stop at the next light and let me out."

Instead, he drove through it, turning left as the signal went from yellow to red. Secretly, he was pleased with her show of pride, but he replied almost casually, "You don't want to go back to that hole in the ground and you know it."

"But I *could* go to St. Timothy's. Father Carmichael would let me stay at the youth hostel, until I found someplace else. He's always been a good friend."

And just where had this model of concern been when she'd been accosted by those thugs? "Tomorrow you can fly to Tibet and commune with the yeti, if that's what you've a mind to do," he shot back, mostly out of the side of his throbbing mouth. "Tonight you're staying where I can be sure that you're warm and safe."

Although he felt her gaze several times after that, she didn't speak to him again until they were on the street where he lived. It suited him fine. He still needed to figure out what he thought he was doing.

"I don't have any of my stuff," she mumbled.

"Define stuff."

"A toothbrush at least."

Worth slowed as he approached his house. "McGuire can supply you with that. I'm confident he can find just about anything you might need."

After parking, he climbed out of the car and joined Rocky. The front door opened and his houseman appeared. Here goes, he thought.

As though she could read his mind, Rocky asked, "How's he going to take this? I mean, you bringing me back here?"

"Not that you can easily notice, but I don't employ McGuire for his opinion."

Surprise and amusement played tug-of-war on his employee's face as they climbed the stairs. "'Tis a sad day when the lasses cease coming quietly, eh, sir?"

Worth touched his bloody handkerchief to his puffy lip
and thought about how satisfying it would be to flatten the
cocky ingrate. Or to remind him that he was one faux pas
away from being shipped back to his homeland—without
references. "Shut up, you fool," he muttered, and ush-
ered Rocky inside.

"Get me an ice pack," he said, removing his topcoat.

"And I'll fill the ice bucket in the study," McGuire
added.

Worth shot him a sidelong look to make sure he wasn't
still being irreverent. Seeing nothing incriminating in his
servant's expression, he grunted his agreement. Then he
turned and motioned to Rocky to remove her coat.

She didn't budge. Her hands thrust deep in her pockets, she stood there as though cast in mortar.

Was it his tuxedo that bothered her? Did it make her feel
ashamed of how her own clothes looked? "Maybe you'd
prefer to warm up first, in which case, feel free to keep the
coat on."

She glanced down at herself and, as though coming to
some conclusion, quickly unbuttoned. That's when Worth
saw what she wore beneath the coat.

It was the sweater he'd given her. Strangely pleased, he
swung back to McGuire, who also stood observing her.
"See that a guest room has everything Miss Grimes might
need for the night."

"Immediately, sir. What about dinner? Since you're
back this early, am I to presume you haven't eaten?"

Worth asked Rocky, "Are you hungry?"

"I... haven't thought much about it."

She looked as though she hadn't had more than a few
bites of anything since he'd last seen her. Aware his injury
would make it too uncomfortable to eat anything himself,
Worth told McGuire, "Bring something into the study for

our guest when you're done upstairs." With a sweep of his hand, he directed Rocky there.

Because he wasn't supposed to be home tonight, there was no cheerful fire lit; however, logs and kindling were set in readiness. Worth slipped off his jacket and lit it.

Rising from his crouched position, he found her still poised for flight in the middle of the room, her hands clasped behind her back. But nerves didn't keep her from staring about her with childlike wonder.

"What do you think?" he asked, yielding to a strong curiosity to know how she felt about his home.

"Have you read all these books?"

The comment intrigued him. He thought she might notice the luxury of the hunter green suede chaise longue, the irreplaceable artwork, the imported rugs or the modest collection of oriental bronzes by the state-of-the-art stereo. But all she seemed to focus on was the ceiling-to-floor bookcases that lined almost every wall in the room.

"Most of them. There are almost as many more upstairs. You're welcome to browse, if you find you can't sleep."

She lifted one shoulder, avoiding his gaze. It was the second time she'd reacted somewhat evasively around the subject of reading. It made him wonder. "*Can* you read?"

Her chin shot up. "Yeah. Sure... sort of." Then she glanced at the shelves again and the fight seeped out of her. "Only not as good as I should. The schools I went to didn't have the greatest teachers, and I was absent a lot because I had to take care of Badger. I dropped out after the eleventh grade."

McGuire appeared with the ice pack and bucket, saving Worth from an immediate need to respond. Grateful for the reprieve, he used the opportunity to digest this latest revelation.

Having grown up in an environment of privilege, he hadn't spent a great deal of time thinking about how tough a life other people may have had. Being raised in an all-male environment had also instilled in him a strong competitive spirit. As a result his attention had always been directed toward his own challenges and successes, first during his school years, then in business as he'd climbed his father's company's corporate ladder. He'd been pushed and coached by a master of the game. What would it have been like to have had none of that?

He took the ice pack from McGuire, brought it to his lip and frowned. No picture materialized.

"Too bulky, sir? I can take it back to the kitchen and crush the ice," McGuire said, pouring Worth his favorite Scotch whisky from the decanter across the room.

"What? No." Worth sat down in his favorite high-back chair. "It's fine. But when you bring the tray, you might bring something for Miss Grimes to drink. Tea?" he asked her. "Hot chocolate?"

She looked at a loss for words again. "I . . . don't want to be any trouble."

As he handed Worth the drink, McGuire looked from him to their guest. "It's no inconvenience, miss. I don't mind saying, I make a lovely hot chocolate with the whipped-cream topping. Much more tasty than that chemical-laced concoction called marshmallow."

Worth could tell by the way she swallowed that a cup of either would leave a huge impression on her. In a mood to spoil her, he said, "The cream, McGuire, and as quickly as you can. We've been through another difficult night." When he was gone, Worth considered the young woman who still stood clearly uncomfortable in the middle of the room. "Why don't you sit down, before you drop."

With a dubious look, she lowered herself to the edge of the nearest chair. Her hesitation reminded him of a child expecting a rebuke of some sort. And yet he was acutely aware that she wasn't a child. He'd seen it with his own eyes and felt it when he'd held her against him. The truth also radiated in the intriguing pools of her midnight eyes.

Troubled, he murmured, "Whatever am I to do with you?"

Immediately, the defensiveness was back in her bearing. "You don't have to *do* anything. Coming here was your idea, not mine. If you've changed your mind and want me to go—"

"I didn't mean to—ouch! *Damn it!*" He had to remember not to enunciate so much. "Just relax, will you? I won't bite."

"Good, 'cause if you tried to, you'd learn I'm one who bites back."

The image of her doing that and then rising on tiptoe to kiss and lick away the sting, sent a sweet, thick flow of warm blood through his body and triggered other thoughts even more disturbing.

Could he be losing his mind? Of all people...not a ragamuffin from the wrong side of town!

But there was no denying it; she'd captured his imagination and wouldn't let go. It defied her coarse manners and couldn't be muted by her oversize, bohemian-style attire. Like it or not, she still bore a striking resemblance to his crystalline *Galatea,* and because of that he wasn't going to find it easy to let her slip out of his life a second time. At least not until he proved something to himself first.

"I don't like it when you stare at me like that."

"If it's any consolation, I'm not thrilled that I find myself doing so."

"You're talking strange again."

"Yes, I suppose I am. Rock—blast. What's your real name?"

"That is my real name. At least it's what everyone's called me most of my life. I think it's much better than what's on my birth certificate."

"Well, I think it's hideous. What's your legal name?"

She made a face. "Roxanne."

"Fascinating."

"Says you. I'm no Roxanne."

He wondered. "Would you like to be?"

Even as she stared at him, clearly befuddled, he realized that he'd been working toward this moment for the last hour. Maybe he'd been planning on it since she slammed the car door in his face on Christmas Eve.

"What if," he began, "I gave you the chances you've missed so far in your life? Clothes, a home, school, exposure to a completely different world from what you've known up until now? Would that interest you?"

She looked more suspicious than shocked. "Why would you do that?"

Careful, he warned himself. It wouldn't do to tell her that he needed to erase an illusion plaguing him, or that he meant to prove a point. She didn't need to understand his desire to convince himself for sanity's sake that there was no living version of what he was seeking. All he had to do was ignore the desire she'd triggered in him with the stealth of an adversary sneaking up in the dark.

"My reasons," he said slowly, "will have to remain my own."

"Sounds fishy to me."

Strange, he'd have thought she would leap at the offer. Would she do nothing expected? "You must want something."

"Sure. Who doesn't?"

"Well, think of the opportunities that would open to you."

"I'd rather hear what this is gonna cost me."

Sensing her interest, but annoyed that she was proving more difficult to convince than he'd anticipated, Worth rose and began pacing. "Your complete dedication, for one thing. Let's face it, your language skills are deplorable, your style of dress worse, and as you've said yourself, your education on a whole is sorely lacking."

"Jeez . . . what do you sound like when you *don't* like somebody?"

"Trust me, you never want to find out." He moved directly before her. "I'm not doing this because I'm a nice man, Roxanne, but for purely selfish reasons. Before long you'll have called me every name imaginable and then some. Truth be known, I don't even expect you to last. But if you *are* willing to apply yourself, I'll be there to help you in every way I can."

She stared at him as though he'd lost his mind. At this point he about had himself convinced; why else, after living as a bachelor for all his adult life, was he inviting a veritable stranger to share his home with him? Especially someone who was clearly going to give him more back talk than McGuire?

"You're serious?"

"Totally."

"If I say yes—and I'm not saying I do yet—I want the right to lock my bedroom door."

"You'd better, or I'll do it for you *and* give the key to McGuire."

Startled, confused, she shook her head. "I don't understand you."

"It's not necessary that you do," he replied, suddenly feeling the weight of his years. "The question is whether or not you want to take advantage of a once-in-a-lifetime opportunity. What's your answer, Roxanne?"

Four

___

Why had she said yes? A week later, as she sat behind Worth's desk and watched him pace before the fireplace, Rocky wondered about that, and about the starch Worth Harrison Drury IV must eat by the spoonful to keep his back and shoulders so damned straight.

The *"IV"...jeez.* When she'd learned that bit of trivia, after he'd handed her one of his gold-embossed business cards, in case she needed to phone him in an emergency, she'd almost choked on her breakfast orange juice. And when she'd heard him say it...he sounded as though he was on the shortlist to the British throne or something. Of course, a week ago, she'd never heard of the term *shortlist.*

"Once more, Roxanne. You'll want to be ready to dive right into your initial foreign language class at college."

"But we're supposed to be concentrating on preparing me for my high school equivalency diploma first," she reminded him, tapping her pencil on the folder of material she felt they should be working on.

"After this hour of language study. Once more—the present, past and future tense of 'I cannot find my wagon.'"

Rocky scowled at the trim but solid silhouette he cut in his burgundy cardigan sweater, the perfectly creased dress slacks and still-crisp white shirt, before refocusing on the book in front of her. He'd worn everything but the sweater to the office; did the man never look wilted? "Who thought up these stupid sentences? No one over the age of five would be caught dead saying them."

"This isn't about content, it's about grammar. What's more, I'd like to remind you that *you* chose Spanish because you already had a smattering of knowledge of it."

"Yeah, and let me tell you that Manny the Moose and Tina Esperanza, not to mention all the other Latinos I know, would bust a gut if I tried talking at them the way this dumb book says to."

"*To. To them,*" Worth replied, enunciating carefully. "And pray tell what degrees do Ms. Esperanza and Mr. Moose hold that make them such experts?"

Rocky burst into laughter. Delighted, she leaned back in the chair and spun it around and around. "Mr. Moose. I love it. The more indignant you get, the funnier, y'know?"

"*Roxanne.*"

His exasperated tone had her uncurling her legs from their Indian-style position to stop the spinning. The added disapproval she saw etched in his sculpted features ended her laughter with a soft "Oops."

"Indeed."

Dear heaven, why did a man with so much going for him see so little to smile about, while she who had next to nothing managed to make her own moments of sunshine? Sometimes, Rocky concluded, life made no sense at all.

But what did was knowing she owed him an apology. Again.

She'd taken Worth up on his offer because she'd recognized this as her one chance to rise out of the rut of her life. He was right; knowledge was power, and she wanted that power so she could change things for herself and for the people she cared about in her old neighborhood. She had to be careful not to lose her focus on that and blow the opportunity of a lifetime.

"I'm sorry," she said solemnly. "But we've worked nonstop all evening. My brain can't do any more present, past, future."

His gaze moved over her face and seemed to linger on her mouth. It gave her a funny, shaky feeling down in the pit of her stomach, so that when he said "All right," she almost lost track of what it was he'd agreed to.

Grateful, Rocky closed the textbook and put it aside. She needed to slow down her imagination and stop thinking she saw more than was there. Sure, Worth was interested in her—like a scientist was interested in a bug under a microscope. It was all in her head that in the last few days he'd had some difficulty in maintaining their student-tutor status.

But, oh, she thought, peering at him from beneath the veil of her lowered lashes, what if he did see her as more than his "experiment"? What would it be like to have those strong, elegant hands slipping under the hem of her sweater and touching her in places...

"Roxanne!"

"Huh? I'm listening," she quickly assured him. She was sure, though, that her cheeks were turning pink from embarrassment. Fortunately, Worth turned his back to her.

"I said for a change we'll spend the last half hour on your diction. While we're at it, we'll see if we can remove such responses like 'Huh?' from your repertoire."

She rolled her eyes thinking she would rather work on her GED stuff. "Can't we do something else? I'm beginning to sound like a frog. Why don't you turn on the stereo instead, and you can teach me the waltz now. You said you would."

"I did nothing of the kind. I said it wouldn't hurt for you to learn some ballroom dancing in case you ever attended a formal event of some kind."

Rocky let Worth correct her, but launched herself across the room to the stereo, anyway. She knew exactly the piece of music she wanted. Not the one that Strauss guy wrote, she thought, ignoring the box already out on the table. She found his work too heavy and formal—much like Worth when he was in his more overbearing moments. No, she preferred the gentler musician, the one that made him get those strange looks in his eyes and made him less regimental around her.

Chopin. She handled the CD with all the care Worth had taught her and painstakingly set it in place. As the first strains of music filled the room, she crossed over to him and executed a deep curtsy as she'd seen an actress do on the late show the other night.

"Very pretty, but American women rarely curtsy these days. Not unless you're being presented formally to society, or you're a diva receiving a standing ovation for a performance."

Rocky was sorry to hear about that. It seemed that everything she liked best about so-called proper behavior was the stuff that was no longer in style. "What if I meet royalty?"

"That remains a judgment call."

"Which means," she said, offering a teasing smile, "that I wasn't entirely wrong, was I, Mr. Worth Drury IV?"

His gaze wandered over her hair, and she could see him fighting a smile. "I see you're determined to be incorrigible tonight."

"Hey! I looked that up today," Rocky said, brightening. "You use it so much around me, I wanted to know why. It took me a while to find it, though. I started in the Es. But McGuire helped straighten me out."

"Shades of the blind leading the blind," Worth drawled.

"He said you've used the word on him a lot, too."

"Far less than he deserves, believe me. As for you, young lady, I wish you would apply yourself as fervently to your other studies as you do toward socializing with my servant."

Rocky wasn't at all put off by his pointed look. "I'd be happy to, if more of what you wanted me to study made some...practical sense to me. But I can't see learning stuff in Spanish for example that I'm never gonna use. Going to use," she amended, even as he cleared his throat to point out her error.

"I'm beginning to believe the early philosophers were right—education *is* wasted on the young."

She wrinkled her nose at him. "Come on, we're wasting the music, Lord Fossil."

With an aggrieved look that somehow seemed feigned, Worth took hold of her hands and showed her how to position them. Then he went through the steps with her. They circled the chairs and couch in the middle of the room, and she soon got the hang of things. It allowed them to increase their speed and keep better time with the music.

"Oh, I wish I was wearing a gown like the actress had on in the movie I watched," Rocky said, her tone wistful.

Worth's smile turned sardonic. "I was wondering how long it would take you to start hinting for gifts."

"I'm not hinting for anything!" Aghast, she stopped watching her feet to stare up at him. "I didn't mean I'd actually want to own one. Jeez, what would I do with it? But I'd like to try one on once. They look so neat, 'cause you can't even see any feet."

"*That's* what appeals to you?" Worth asked, looking puzzled.

"Sure. Then no one could tell when you made a mistake." She *always* was making a mistake. Too bad they didn't have something that worked as well for the mouth.

"A good partner would always know if you erred," Worth murmured, just as she barely shortchanged a step.

Rocky groaned. "How could you tell that time? It wasn't as though I missed any beats."

"But I could feel the way your body went rigid for a moment. Even though I wasn't watching your feet, I can feel it here," he said, subtly shifting the hand at her waist to stroke her back. "And here," he added, his fingers tightening around her left hand.

A current of awareness shot through her and scorched a path of electricity through her body. "Oh. Right," she replied, her brief laugh sounding breathless and nervous to her own ears. Good grief, she thought, disgusted with her reaction. It wasn't as though he'd groped her or anything.

But his gentleness, combined with his lingering touch, made her palm suddenly turn damp. Abruptly, she pulled free and rubbed it against her new, blue wool slacks. Worth had ordered them and her matching sweater by phone for her, then sent McGuire to collect them the day after New Year's.

"I don't know how they did this in the old days without getting sweaty hands," she said, regretting that she'd ever suggested they attempt this. On the other hand, Worth seemed disgustingly unaffected.

"Oh, they got sweaty palms. They just wore gloves or used hankies to hide it. For all their formality back then, there was no denying that dancing was as much a sexual courting ritual as it was a social communication device. The difference between then and now is that today people blatantly use their bodies to signal what's on their minds."

"Sounds more honest to me."

"If copulation for the sake of survival of the species is the bottom line, perhaps." Worth took hold of her hand again. "But there was a time when people saw lovemaking as one of the few behavioral traits that separated us from animals."

As they began dancing again, Rocky decided she didn't know enough about such things. She just knew that so far, she'd had little to do with the opposite sex because she'd never felt a strong enough urge to bother. At least not enough to take the risks that seemed so life threatening in this day and age.

"Have I embarrassed you?"

Worth's low, sexy baritone interrupted her somber thoughts. "No," she replied, again feeling heat spreading through her. It was the dancing, she told herself. They were dancing faster now, and it took more energy and concentration. Despite being in good shape, her heart was beginning to pound as though she'd sprinted to the harbor and back. "Shoot, I know about sex," she tossed back, determined to prove she could be nonchalant, too.

As soon as she spoke, she stumbled.

They were going to fall. She felt herself pulling Worth off balance. In the next instant he lifted her against him and used his powerful body to keep them both upright until he braced himself against the side of one bookcase.

That's what you get for underestimating his strength and agility.

That and then some, she realized as the maneuver brought them nose to nose, eye to eye, and... Oh, God, she thought, moistening her lips. Mouth to mouth.

As their breaths mingled, their bodies grew very still and tense. Rocky became aware of her breasts swelling, hardening, then Worth's taut stomach muscles, thighs...all of him, changing. Deep inside, her heart thrummed against rib bones that suddenly seemed too tight a constraint.

Unable to help herself, she dropped her gaze from the eyes boring into hers to focus on his mouth. Like hers, his lips were slightly parted, his breath shallow. Suddenly he'd become a far different man from the one he'd been letting her see. Also different from the gentle man she sometimes sensed beneath the aloof, polished exterior. To discover who this Worth Drury was, all she needed to do was to turn her head slightly, lean forward, and—

"That's one lesson I won't teach you."

His words were clipped, but they were contradicted by the fire heating his normally cool gray eyes. No, she decided, she wouldn't let him confuse her this time.

"Who's asking you to?" she heard herself snap back.

"You are. It's obvious in every inch of your face."

"Maybe you should look in a mirror sometime and see what's on your own, professor."

The arm around her waist tightened, becoming as resolute as a steel band. "Don't flirt with me, Roxanne."

"I was making an observation."

"One full of challenge."

The room should have hummed from the tension building between them. But Rocky refused to back down, although she did wonder at her nerve. This was the last man to go toe-to-toe with, so what was it about his brooding good looks that mesmerized her so...even as he provoked her?

Every night when she snuggled deep in her plush, queen-size bed, she warned herself that all this luxury and comfort was going to mean blessed little once he broke her heart. And she sensed he would. If not one way, then another.

But it didn't change anything. The same hunch that told her he didn't have a clue as to what happiness was all about, told her that this was a man who could teach her about passion. And wanted to. Why he should be interested in her, she had no idea, but the truth burned in him. She could feel it, just as she could feel her own rising temperature, and it made it all the more difficult to resist her eagerness to learn more about him.

"Little fool. You don't know the first thing about what you're inviting."

The sudden muscle spasm in his left cheek, more than his words, signaled she'd pushed too hard. Then he closed his mouth over hers, and she stopped noticing anything but the sensations he taught her.

How could she have called him cold, aloof? He was more like a flash fire, surrounding her and consuming her in a matter of heartbeats. No, she had no experience with anything like this; but captivated, she tightened her arms around his neck and went willingly into the adventure.

His mouth was hard, possessive, his tongue demanding. Within seconds he'd doubled, then tripled her knowledge of kissing and began racing her through a crash course in seduction. Each new stroke, each hot caress drew a new and different reaction from her, until every nerve in her body hummed and every muscle trembled with excitement and yearning.

At that moment he could have lowered her onto the couch, the carpet, and she would have gone willingly. He wanted to. His aroused body made that obvious. But a muffled cough from the doorway put an embarrassing end to that fantasy.

Worth swore under his breath; however, he shifted so that his back was to McGuire and she was all but hidden by his greater size. Rocky thought his protectiveness touching.

"What?" he growled over his shoulder.

Fascinating, she thought, noticing the moisture that beaded on his forehead. She would never have expected a man so in control, to break out in a sweat over a few kisses. *She,* of course, would have been a puddle on the floor if it wasn't for his firm hold of her waist. But to see Worth in this condition was food for the mind.

"Excuse me, sir, but what refreshments will you want for this evening's lesson?"

Good grief, Rocky thought, was it nine already? Every evening Worth ended their lessons with an hour of instruction in a more formal etiquette: how to serve tea, making polite small talk, using the day's teachings to filter them into useful practice. She didn't see that much was rubbing off on her, but she enjoyed the crumpets, as McGuire called them.

To her surprise Worth replied, "We won't require anything. Miss Grimes will be retiring early tonight."

As McGuire withdrew, Rocky continued to study him, not at all liking the vibes she began to pick up from him. He was getting angry. Why?

"Is this what they call being banished to one's room?" she asked him.

"Your acumen is growing in leaps and bounds tonight."

Rocky eased out of his hold. "You're serious. I'm dismissed?"

Worth moved, too. He started toward his desk, only to spin around again and point at her. "Don't you ever play with me again, or I promise you I'll send you back to that miserable pit you came from. In the future stick to toying with boys of your own caliber."

Stung by humiliation, Rocky wanted to run upstairs and hide, but she knew she had to stand her ground if she was to keep the last dredges of her self-respect. "Are you suggesting this was all my fault?" she demanded, closing the space between them.

"Whose then?"

"*You're* the one who brought up sex."

"You're the one who was flaunting it in my face."

She swung out, but not with the intent to land a ladylike slap. Boiling mad, she curled her fingers into a tight fist, aching to deliver a one-swing, knockout punch. Fortunately for him, Worth's reflexes were as sharp as his tongue, and she didn't get close.

Red-faced and steely-eyed, he rasped, "Try that again and this arrangement is over."

"As far as I'm concerned, it is!" Rocky snapped, feeling tears of fury threatening. Determined she wouldn't give him the satisfaction of seeing them fall, she raced from the room.

Jackass. Worth raked his hand through his hair. *Imbecile.* He'd had no business taking off her head, not when he was the one to blame for letting things go too far.

Merciful heaven. His body still throbbed with the unsatisfied craving to know more, all of her. She'd amazed him. How could one small woman contain so much passion? Allowing that the kiss should never have happened, there was no denying that none had ever affected him so fast or so deeply.

Kiss, hell. That had been a foundation rattler.

He had the strongest urge to run. An equally powerful urge tempted him to race upstairs and finish what they'd begun.

What to do? The wisest thing, of course, would be to send her packing. But fairness didn't allow him to consider that option. Why slam the door on whatever it was that she wanted for her future because he'd suddenly discovered a problem in his ability to control himself? Besides, she was making impressive progress. He tried not to let her get too excited over it, since a great deal of work remained ahead of them. But if she applied herself, her limitations were her own to plot.

If only she wasn't so stubborn, so prone toward mutinous behavior. If only she wasn't so damned desirable.

Sweet torment, from now on he had to be more careful. Knowing he could be intoxicated by her taste, her softness, her willingness to let him do what he would with her, he had to make sure it never happened again. What's more, he owed her an apology.

He climbed the stairs, the weight of his task heavy on his shoulders. Even before he reached the top, he could hear the turmoil in her room—drawers slamming, doors banging. Searching for the clothes she'd arrived in no doubt. Worth had confiscated them personally and had ordered McGuire to dispose of them any way possible.

Reaching her door, he knocked. Immediately everything went still inside. Then came a sniff, a crash and a curse. Finally he heard a hesitant "McGuire?"

"It's me, Roxanne. Open up."

"Dream on, professor," she snapped, all hesitancy gone from her voice.

"I'd like to talk to you, and I prefer to do it face-to-face. Now, please . . . unlock the door. I'm not leaving until you do."

At first he thought she might ignore him, anyway, but after a short pause he heard the click and then the door opened. She stood to the side of it, refusing to look at him. He could understand why; she would no more like to be seen with a tear-streaked face than he'd wanted to know he'd made her cry merely with words.

Stepping inside to make certain he could say his piece without having the door slammed in his face, Worth clasped his hands behind his back to keep from brushing away a lingering tear. "Are you all right?"

"Don't think this is for you," she muttered, wiping her cheeks with the cuffs of her sweater. "I slammed my hand in a drawer."

"Would you like me to look at it?"

"No."

"Would you like McGuire to bring you something? Ice or some aspirin?"

"No! You *shall* say whatever you came to say, and then get lost so I can finish."

The blue velvet ribbon she'd used to tie back her hair was coming loose, and Worth caught it as she pushed past him. "What if I told you I wanted to apologize?"

She spun around and tried to snatch the length of material out of his hand. "Stuff it."

Worth tightened his grip. "You're hurt and you're angry, I understand."

"You don't know anything about how I feel, so don't you dare try to give me a Drury lecture about how you do. And give me that," she demanded, finally securing a grip on the ribbon. "I must have been crazy to believe this could've worked."

"It can. It will." Using his greater strength, Worth used her hold to jerk her toward him. He kept her from stumbling against him by grasping her shoulders. "Roxanne, listen to me. I'm accepting full blame. I let things go too far, that's all."

"The trouble with your game, Mr. Worth Drury IV, is that you don't know what you want the rules to be."

"This is not a game." He struggled to ignore the pleasure it gave him to touch her. "And I know what the rules are. I just chose not to pay attention, because I had to know how your mouth felt under mine."

She stopped struggling and stared at him.

He allowed a crooked smile. "What did you expect, a lie?"

"A gold-plated one."

Worth drew in a deep breath and let the insult go. He figured she deserved another hit or two under the circumstances. "Feel better now that you've got that one out of your system?"

"No." She looked away. "You hurt me."

"Yes. I don't expect you to understand why... I'm not certain that I do myself. Suffice it to say that opening to people, trusting, isn't what I do well. Today you had a bitter taste of what that feels like."

Rocky nodded and considered him for several serious seconds. "How long do your affairs usually last?"

"My— I don't see that that's any of your business." Maybe he sounded a bit thin-skinned, but he'd expected an entirely different response than the one she'd given him.

"It is, if I'm going to be judged against every woman who's disappointed you."

He took his time, relaxed before answering. "You're not going to be judged, because you and I aren't going to have that kind of relationship."

"You mean your curiosity's been satisfied?"

When she lifted one of those fine, arched eyebrows of hers, her face took on a maturity and allure Worth found even more disturbing than her anger. "I'm saying that I don't have to walk in front of a speeding train to know it would be bad for my health."

"Is that what you call a backhanded compliment?"

"No, it's an analysis of how I underestimated our chemistry. Now," Worth said, turning away because the surprise softening her eyes made his insides twist with new hunger, "have we cleared up this misunderstanding?"

"We didn't have a misunderstanding, we had a fight."

"Roxanne..."

"All right. I'm not quitting. But," she added, circling him so that he had to look at her, "I won't stop speaking my mind."

"I never doubted it." Relief, he discovered, almost made him light-headed. In self-defense he pivoted and headed for the door. "By the way," he said over his shoulder, "I've decided to take tomorrow off. It's time we added to your wardrobe. Then we'll have lunch in town and put some of your lessons to the test."

"I'll try not to embarrass you by slurping my soup."

"No, you'll probably high-five the parking valet instead."

Worth left the room feeling better, her wry humor almost succeeding in removing the concern that had forced him to go upstairs. Almost, but not entirely; for despite having survived this temptation, Worth knew it would take more, all his willpower, to endure another.

* * *

"Pink? You want me to wear *pink?*" Rocky stared at Worth as he nodded to the sales attendant holding yet another dress to carry into the dressing room for her. She turned her back to the blonde, who looked at Worth as though she wouldn't mind modeling for him herself, and whispered, "You've gotta be joking."

"That particular hue is called rose and it's an excellent color for you."

"Why don't you dip me in cupcake frosting, already!" Rocky scanned the offerings in the showroom, until her gaze fell upon something far more interesting. She hurried over to the rack and snatched up a two-piece leather suit in poppy red. "Now take a look at this. *This* is what I call an outfit."

"Add the rose dress to the others," Worth said to the attendant. "She'll be right in to try them on."

With a mournful sigh, Rocky put back the leather. If only he would let her try it on, she had a hunch she would have no problem changing his mind. "Okay, it's your money."

"The dress will be perfect for the art gallery showing I told you I'd be taking you to in two weeks. If you went in the leather, everyone would think I found you by dialing 1-900-Yumm."

"Make me wear the pink and they still will...only they'll suspect you of a worse fetish."

Worth laughed softly. "Nice try, but it won't work. Now, come along to the gowns. I prefer to choose one without that barracuda stalking me."

Delighted by his laugh and relieved that he wasn't fooled by the woman's practiced smile and solicitous manner, Rocky followed him to the next section in the store. A gown? Where did he plan to take her that she needed one?

On impulse she snatched up the first frilly thing to catch her eye. Banana-yellow taffeta and lace. "Oh, look! How did they know we were coming?"

"Don't be a sore loser. Let me show you what grace under pressure can yield. Here, hold this one against you."

Glancing over to see what he'd chosen for her, Rocky thrust the yellow back on the rack. She couldn't believe her eyes. He'd picked out a one-shouldered sheath in midnight blue silk with a starburst of silver adorning the sleeve. It was cut to follow the body with every movement, and flare gently just below the hips. Did he really think she could pull off wearing such a creation? she wondered, clutching it possessively to her.

"That's the one. It matches your eyes."

His words were matter-of-fact, but Rocky didn't care. All she heard was that he'd attributed her eyes with having such a mysterious, deep color. "I'm going to try this on first," she whispered, stroking it reverently.

"No. Keep it for last."

"But—"

"Last."

Muttering about bossy men, she headed for the dressing room.

A half hour later, as she spun between Worth and the three-sided mirror, she decided maybe he knew something about dressing a woman after all. The suits and dresses she'd tried were what he'd called classic. All she knew was that they gave her a feeling of maturity and femininity. What's more, she couldn't wait to wear the pantsuits to the classes he seemed so certain were in her future. Even the pink outfit was okay.

But nothing was as wonderful as the gown—or Worth's expression when she emerged from the fitting room wearing it. It might as well have been made for her. She saw it as his eyes turned smoky and his whole body went still and very controlled. Never had she felt more beautiful or aware.

She laughed, twirling again for him so he could get the full effect of the graceful flow of the skirt. "Isn't it breathtaking?"

"Breathtaking."

"With a good haircut, maybe to her shoulders, she'll look charming," the attendant added with a tight smile. "If you like, I can recommend a superb stylist who works miracles."

"No one's touching her hair."

Rocky froze and stared at his reflection in one of the mirrors. She'd never heard that edge in his voice before. Not even yesterday, when he'd been angry with her.

"Of course," the woman said quickly, "it's not unattractive down. She looks rather...exotic in a way."

Worth didn't reply. He merely took out one of his business cards and handed it to the woman. "Send the bill to my office. Roxanne, I'll wait for you in the front."

She would have been hurt if she hadn't seen him swallow. Only then did she understand.

He still wants me. He wants me.

Her heart threatened to leap up her throat from the wonder of it.

"Not exactly full of compliments, is he?" the woman muttered under her breath.

"You have to recognize them when you hear them." Humming softly, Rocky waltzed into the dressing room.

A short while later, wearing the pink dress as a gesture, she sat across from him at the garden restaurant in one of Boston's skyscrapers. Too enthralled to pay attention to the menu, she gazed around the lush plants, the orchids and fountains in open wonder.

"Are you planning to read your menu by telepathy?" Worth asked, not bothering to glance up from his.

"Oh, don't growl. I only want to take it all in. This has to be the most fantastic thing I've ever seen—next to your house, of course."

One corner of his mouth twitched. "Of course."

"Is it going to be disgustingly expensive? You've already dropped a bundle on the clothes."

"Disgustingly. I expect you to enjoy every bite."

"I'll try."

He glanced up then, and she beamed at him. It seemed to take him off guard, and he hastily refocused on his menu. So, Rocky mused, opening her own copy, the man was normal after all. Then she gasped.

"What's wrong?"

"No wonder they can afford to have so many waiters for each table. Some of this stuff costs more than I earned in a day of dishwashing!"

"The first order of business when we get home," Worth drawled, continuing his perusal, "is to focus on your deplorable affection for the word *stuff*."

"Okay. Say... if it turns out that I can't eat everything I order, do you think they'd be insulted if I asked for a doggie bag?"

About to reach for his water glass, Worth nearly tipped it over. Obviously, nothing so common had ever happened to him before because he turned beet red. "I'd find it highly unusual for you to find that you'd need to," he wheezed, reaching for the glass again.

"Why?"

"Because... this is a *French* restaurant, Roxanne."

She shook her head, still not catching his drift. "What's that supposed to mean?"

"I'll explain it to you later," he said, and ducked behind his menu.

Five

"Okay, explain this. I've seen better stuff by kids in my neighborhood, who mostly use a spray can." Roxanne whispered, frowning at the paint-splattered canvas that took up most of one wall at the gallery.

Worth took a sip of his champagne, even though he didn't usually care for the wine. It bought him the time he needed to think of a proper response, as he was inclined to do more and more these days when responding to her. "I believe it was Tolstoy who said, 'Art is not a handicraft, it is the transmission of feeling the artist has experienced.'"

"In that case, this poor guy needs a vacation from his reality. A long one, like in a padded cell."

Worth placed his hand beneath her elbow and directed her away from the piece. "Are you trying to tell me that you're not enjoying this exhibit?"

Her answering smile was as full of mischief as her tone was airy. "Nonsense. I'm having a delightful time. Only that quote makes no more sense than the less-is-more lecture you gave me after we got out of that French restaurant a few weeks ago. I still believe that if they served decent-size portions, instead of all those bite-size ones, they wouldn't have ended up with so many plates to wash and *I* wouldn't have gotten sick afterward.''

"You got ill from not only devouring your own rich dessert, but mine as well."

Roxanne tapped her rolled program against his shoulder. "That's an indelicate technicality to point out to a lady, Mr. Drury."

Worth chuckled into his glass, enjoying her mimicry of the practiced conversations going on around them. Secretly in agreement, and not seeing much use for either the painting or the artist she'd criticized, he found it more entertaining to let her think otherwise. He'd come to enjoy their verbal skirmishes too much.

Six weeks, he thought, guiding her toward the next room, and he had yet to tire of the challenge she presented. Her mind was quick, her spirit strong, and her energy inspiring. Skirmishes aside, she'd applied herself well to her studies, gaining her high school equivalency diploma within weeks. A few days ago, despite the fact that the second semester had already begun, Worth had pulled strings to get her admitted at the university. Although understandably intimidated, so far it seemed she'd missed so much that she'd slipped too far behind the rest of her class. But then he'd established strict rules to make sure she spent as much time studying as possible. And he continued working with her regularly. He enjoyed the sessions too much to give them up. Yet. Even though she'd nicknamed him The Dictator. He could live with that. It was the idea of living without her—and every day he made a point to remind himself that it was inevitable, eventually—that was beginning to give him difficulties.

"Oh...look."

Her awed whisper put a welcome end to his brooding and resurrected the pleasure he always felt in her company. Glad to see she'd spotted what he'd intended to show her next, Worth led her to the glass sculpture in the middle of the room. The figure was of a swan with its wings spread ready for flight and its neck arched. A remarkable achievement; however, rather than focus on the piece, Worth watched Roxanne. Her expression bordered the spiritual and fascinated him, as did the way she began to reach out to it, only to realize what she was doing and stop herself.

"It's...is *extraordinary* the word I want?"

"Yes." He watched her circle the piece, the light beneath the crystal illuminating her face and the glossy cascade of her hair. "*Extraordinary* may be the only word."

"I've never seen anything closer to perfect."

"You find yourself looking for a flaw because the very idea of such perfection is almost painful."

"Not to me. It makes me feel...glad to be alive."

"Encouraging more hero worship, bro?"

Although he'd expected to meet a number of acquaintances this afternoon, Worth found the taunting, familiar voice the most unwelcome of intrusions to follow Roxanne's bittersweet spontaneity. Turning, he faced his younger brother, who, despite his droll query, seemed eager to do some worshipping of his own.

"Is it the lighting in this place, or have you taken to robbing cradles these days?"

"Go to hell, Chase."

Hardly intimidated, Chase Drury winked at him before circling the swan and awarding a watchful Roxanne his most winning smile. "Good Lord, you are lovely. Worth, old man, I think I'm finally impressed with your taste."

"And I think you'd better stay away from the champagne," Worth replied, adding just enough censure to his voice to let his brother know he wasn't to overstay his welcome. "You're embarrassing my guest."

His fairer-haired sibling ignored him, instead taking possession of Roxanne's left hand. "Allow me to introduce myself. I'm that staid relic's charming and debonair brother. Chase Martel Drury, very willingly at your service, Miss...?"

"Roxanne Grimes," Worth supplied without enthusiasm.

"But my friends call me Rocky," she added.

Worth's mood soured further as he noted the delighted grin breaking out on her face. In her pink suit, with a water-garden oil painting adding an atmospheric backdrop, she epitomized springtime and bliss. A wholly dark, unbearably violent feeling of possessiveness sliced through him.

"Enchanting." Chase touched his lips to her fingers. "Count me in for a lifetime membership in the club."

Now his brother knew the feel of her skin. That it carried the scent of jasmine, the fragrance she seemed to prefer from all those he'd had McGuire supply her with. It was all Worth could do not to bury his fist in his brother's photogenic face. What was happening to him?

Oblivious or indifferent to his discomfort, Chase continued, "Where on earth did my *much* older brother find you?"

"In the gutter." The twinkling of her eyes indicated Roxanne was willing to play, too.

As expected, Chase looked dumbfounded.

"That's where I landed when he ran into me."

"I've tried to warn him about reading the paper while walking on the sidewalk," Chase said, apologetic.

"Oh, he wasn't walking, he was driving."

Shooting Worth an astounded glance, he asked, "Is she serious?"

"She's failing to point out that it was an accident. Isn't there someone waiting for you somewhere, Chase?"

The blue-gray eyes inherited from their mother along with the rest of his coloring, gleamed with irreverence. "Not today, I'm—on the wagon, as it were." Then he turned back to Roxanne. "I'd sue the beast if I were you. He's filthy rich. Never would miss the money, though that damned pride of his would be bent all out of shape."

Roxanne shook her head. Worth wanted to believe she looked at his sibling as though he was an overgrown child. It helped him resist grabbing Chase by the scruff of the neck and tossing him out, regardless of the scene it would cause.

"It wouldn't be right," she told him. "Mad as I was at the time—excuse me, *angry,* I wasn't all that badly hurt. Besides, your brother's been super to me."

"He would be the first to tell you that our father raised only one fool." Once again Chase faced him. "I see her in pearls myself. Sapphires would, of course, bring out those terrific eyes. But pearls against that skin . . ."

"I don't want expensive jewelry," Roxanne declared.

Chase took a step back. "Why not?"

"Because he's already done so much for me."

The wickedness returned to Chase's eyes. "I've never quite heard it put that way before, but—"

"So help me, Chase," Worth began.

"He's financing my education."

"Textbooks instead of Tiffany's," mused Chase, "now there's a new technique I would never have considered."

"That's only part of it. He's giving me free room and board. Believe me, for someone like me to have the privilege of living in the brownstone—"

"You mean he's installed you *in* his home?"

Worth almost groaned out loud. Of all people to share that bit of information with. But it was his own fault; he should have discussed with Roxanne how they would explain their arrangement to anyone who asked. Now his brother would go out of his way to inform their father—who wouldn't take to the idea at all—and then Chase would spill the news to the world at large, starting with the paper's most notorious gossip columnist.

His brother eyed him with a new curiosity. "What's this, bro?"

"Don't read more into this than you should," Worth warned.

"Why not? Not even Erica ever spent more than one night under your roof, and the consensus was that you'd have married her."

Ignoring him, Worth said to a now-subdued Roxanne, "We'd better move along if we're going to make our dinner reservation."

"Sure. Whatever you say. Which way do you—"

"Stop! Don't move," Chase injected, his dark eyes widening as he stared at Roxanne, who'd raised her hand to her hair. "My word. It's remarkable."

"What is?"

She took a cautionary step backward, almost walking into a waiter with a tray of freshly poured champagne. Worth reached out and saved her, but had to resist the impulse to replace his empty glass for a full one.

"The similarities between you and *her,*" Chase said.

Roxanne looked from Chase to him, and Worth decided there was no avoiding some explanation. "I collect this artist's work," he said, with a curt nod at the swan. "I think my brother is implying that you bear a resemblance to one of those pieces."

"You know damned well that's what I was referring to, just as I'm certain you're aware it's more than a resemblance, old son. She could have inspired the piece." His brother studied Roxanne through narrowed eyes. "He hasn't told you about *Galatea?* No, I can see he hasn't. Aren't you playing with something that's likely to explode in your face, Junior?"

"If you don't want to spend a small fortune on plastic surgery for yours," Worth replied as smoothly, "I suggest you take this opportunity to recall a previously scheduled appointment."

"Ah. Of course. Never let it be said I don't know when it's timely to beat a hasty retreat." Laughter made Chase's golden handsomeness all the more irritating as he took Roxanne's hand again. "I'd love to continue this conversation sometime. Perhaps over lunch?"

"That would be—"

"Unlikely," Worth said, before she could finish. "Don't forget your studies, Roxanne."

Chase tisked away the warning. "At the same time, don't forget what they say about all work and no play." Chase bent and kissed her cheek. "We'll talk soon. Ciao, love."

As he strolled away, a long-limbed, lazy, golden cat, Roxanne stared. "What was that all about?"

"Nothing worth wasting any more time on. Shall we go?"

"Go? As in leave? But we haven't seen half of the exhibit yet."

Worth set his empty glass on the next passing tray. "I've seen enough."

"All right. Whatever you say."

Roxanne's docile response would normally have made him suspicious, but now he was simply grateful. Taking hold of her arm, he directed her toward the nearest exit. "Thank you," he muttered under his breath.

"You're welcome."

They retrieved their coats and reached the front exit. Worth held open the door for her. That's when he saw her withdrawn expression. Had he hurt her? How? His annoyance had been directed toward Chase and only him... hadn't it?

"This isn't about you, Roxanne," he told her, not as confident as he had been.

"You don't owe me an explanation. Surely you can think of some philosopher who said, 'He who foots the bill makes all the rules.'"

Worth sighed, his breath visible in the crisp February air, as he lengthened his strides to keep up with her. "You're angry."

"But I have no right to be, do I? There was never anything said about being treated as an equal, whether I learned to get my grammar straight and keep my fingernails clean or not."

Worth handed his ticket over to the parking attendant and waited until the young man had dashed off before replying. "That's a low blow."

"I come from the streets, Worth," she retorted, a faint quiver entering her voice. "When I get pushed too hard, or get hurt too deep, I fall back on survivalist fighting. If you don't like it, tough bananas."

The attendant eased the car up to the curb. Roxanne hurried to it and got in before Worth could assist her, leaving him to tip the valet and climb in behind the wheel.

Only after he was turning onto the street did he trust himself to reply.

"My brother and I have a difficult relationship. I'm afraid you got caught in the middle of that."

"Too bad. He seems like a lot of fun."

"He's thirty years old and there isn't a serious bone in his body, and you'd do well to remember that. Believe me, for all his smooth delivery, the man's never gotten close to a woman before in his life."

"I believe you," Roxanne said, running a hand over her skirt. "Because I happen to think it takes one to know one."

He nearly rear-ended a taxi that was stopping for a traffic light. "What's that supposed to mean?"

"Oh, your styles may be different, but face it, Worth, at your core you're both snobs. And beneath all that attitude, I think you're both afraid of being rejected."

"How impressive. You haven't even enrolled in a psychology class yet, and already you're handing out psychoanalysis."

"I grew up around more men than women. After a while some things start to sink in." She shifted to face him. "Tell me about your relationship with your mother."

Worth gripped the steering wheel tighter. "She has nothing to do with any of this."

"You never speak of her. There's no picture of her in your house. McGuire's never heard her name mentioned—"

"You and McGuire are discussing me behind my back?" He knew they appeared to be getting along like fraternal twins and that a certain amount of exchanging information was inevitable, but this?

"I didn't give him a choice." Roxanne offered a coaxing smile. "You know what a bad time I gave him until he stopped trying to feed me oatmeal."

"Don't remind me."

"But he didn't have much information, so don't blame him for my..."

"Tenacity."

"Whatever."

Worth considered what she'd said. What was wrong with her knowing? It wasn't any great secret, or even a tragedy. It was just...life.

"My mother abandoned us when I was seven and Chase was two," he said, as though reciting his phone number. "She'd met an Italian count who raced cars for a hobby, and decided he offered her more excitement than we did. Six months later they were both killed when he drove off the northern Apennines on their way from Rome to Milan."

"That's...so sad."

He'd long since shut the door on his grief. "She made her choice."

"She rejected her babies." Roxanne fisted her hands over her chic leather bag. "Like Chase, I was luckier, I think, in that I lost my mother when I was younger. I can barely remember her face."

"What happened?"

"She drank, too. That's why I don't. I'm terrified that what consumed them will get me. Mama...drifted away. Sometimes she stayed gone for days at a time. Then it became weeks. One day she never came back. I have no idea how she supported herself. I try not to think about it."

"What about your father?"

She shook her head, her expression blank. "I have no idea. If my mother knew him, she never told Badger. Kinda embarrassing, huh?"

Worth made a turn, relieved that the sun finally crept out from behind the clouds, despite edging near the horizon. He wanted the sting in his eyes. It gave him an excuse to blink several times.

He didn't want to feel. Not this much. Especially not about her. Not for the hurt she covered, not for the shame she thought might tarnish her chances. Not anything. If he ever began...no. He liked his life the way it was. Contained. Controlled.

But curiosity refused to release him. "Why did you tell me? I have a feeling it's not a story you volunteer to many people."

"I told you because I wanted you to see that on the outside we may be very different, but on the inside we all have scars."

She made him feel like a class A rat. Self-possessed. Rigid. Quite different from the way he saw himself. "I have a feeling you're going to be terrifying in a few years," he murmured.

"By then you'll think it's a nice change over annoying."

Her soft laugh warmed him as much as the sun and seduced him...more than he realized, when he heard himself confess, "I also reacted the way I did because I was jealous of Chase."

"I know."

His concentration blown, Worth was grateful to have reached the restaurant's parking lot. Braking and shutting off the engine, he eyed her warily. "Do you?"

Roxanne nodded. "I have to admit it's flattering, too. I haven't exactly been overwhelmed with that kind of attention before. Of course, I've never looked like this before, either."

She swung her gaze away to watch the sunset. He studied her profile burnished by the sun.

"I gave you my word," he said, for his sake as much as hers, "I have no intention of carrying our . . . arrangement beyond the boundaries already set."

"I believe you meant that. But I'm changing, Worth. So are you."

"Are you suggesting I may not be able to control myself?" It was a foolish question. They were so close that when she finally met his gaze again, he found himself in a struggle to fight the allure of her dark eyes, so unfairly fringed with a romantic sweep of lush lashes.

"I don't have to. You want to kiss me right now," she whispered.

He thirsted with the need. But his pride held him back. "Do I? Or is that what you want?"

"Lord Fossil, if I wanted you to kiss me, I'd have already made that clear myself." And with that, Roxanne closed the distance between them and touched her lips to his.

For not being a passionate kiss, Worth couldn't believe his body's intense response. Lured by her softness and her scent, he immediately slipped his hand behind her head and drew her closer. At the same time he parted her lips with his and deepened their kiss to one of exploration.

Hunger struggled for and won its release. With a groan, he yielded to its power, and the kiss grew more demanding. He forgot where they were. He forgot his promise to her and himself. He only knew the fierce craving to have more.

Roxanne's soft moan proved as stimulating as the slide of her fingers over his coat, his tie, his shirt. He wanted her touch. He wanted to explore her, too, to lay her back on the seat and cover her body with his until every inch of her sweet body was imprinted with his own. Then explore...her breasts, so delicate and firm. His hands ached to learn their shape, his mouth watered to discover her creamy taste. Already aroused, his body throbbed to bury itself inside her. Only the reminder of where they were kept the madness in check.

He tore his mouth free and stared at her. "This is insane."

"We both wanted it."

Desire clawed at him. "That doesn't make it right."

"Why?"

Why indeed? He forced himself to release her and sit back in his seat. Slowly the red tide of unsated need receded, and reason returned. "You're living under my roof. In another century you'd be like my ward."

"Whoopee. We're not related, and I'm not underage."

He didn't want to think about age. He didn't want to be reminded of the moral obligation that went along with what he'd taken on. He didn't want to think about how good it had felt to have her in his arms, to touch her, to plumb the sweet depths of her mouth and feel her excitement as her tongue tangled against his with honest, inexperienced desire.

Inexperienced ...

Worth shut his eyes tight. "Your first time should be with someone you love."

"I see. Now you're speaking from experience?"

He deserved the chiding he heard in her voice; however, he couldn't let it change anything. Without answering, he pulled the key from the ignition. "We may be a bit early, but they have a wonderful piano player on weekends in the lounge."

A short, bitter laugh cut through the heavy silence. "You can be such a hypocrite, Worth." She drew in a long breath. "My first time should be with someone who cared that it *would* be the first time. Please take me back to the house. I've lost my appetite."

"Can we talk?"

It seemed as though she'd waited for hours for Worth to leave for work so she could corner McGuire. She hadn't had the opportunity on Monday when she'd had early classes, but today she didn't have to go in until later.

Already dressed in her favorite burgundy pantsuit, she gave the Englishman her most winning smile. She hardly minded that he eyed her across the center work station with more trepidation than welcome. As she'd explained to Worth, this wasn't the first time she'd come down to talk to him.

"I need your help."

McGuire liked to think of himself as a forensic scientist of food. The one thing he didn't like to discuss was his employer. The only thing Rocky wanted to discuss with him was Worth.

After Sunday's episode in the car, Worth had made a point of avoiding her. During their study sessions Sunday and Monday nights, he'd worked especially hard to keep the focus of attention on the business at hand, avoiding anything that could lead to a provocative statement or too much intimacy.

Considering the kiss they'd shared, Rocky considered that as telling as graffiti on building walls.

"Is something wrong, Miss Roxanne?"

She rolled her eyes at the name. "When he's not around, do you think you could call me Rocky?"

"Oh, I don't think he'd approve."

"What—does he have the place wired? Does he make you enter a confessional every night when he comes home? Let's check the microwave. Maybe there's a receiver in there that we don't know about."

"Mr. Drury has a right to his rules, Miss."

"Oh, sure. But let me ask you, do *you* like being called McGuire as though it was a social security number?"

"I..." The slender man sighed. "It's traditional that servants be called by their surname."

"That sounds swell, but what if your surname was...was...Fishbreath or something? What would you rather be called then?"

The Englishman's expression turned worried, then pensive. "Why, I suppose..." He brightened. "How about Rafe?"

"Is that your first name?" she asked hopefully.

"No." He ducked his head and smiled sweetly. "It's Eugene. But you were discussing hypotheticals, and it just so happens that I'm particularly fond of a character on the series 'Love's Law.'"

Not much of a TV buff, Rocky had no idea about the program, but her heart went out to the strange little man, anyway. "Tell you what, I'll call you Rafe if you'll call me Rocky. But only when we're alone," she added, seeing doubt creep into his expression once again.

The tips of the suddenly shy man's ears turned crimson. "That would be jolly fun, but confusing. I'd forget, and Mr. Drury would be angry. Was there something else that you needed, Miss—Rocky?"

She reached across the center counter and stilled him as he turned to the refrigerator. "I'm not asking you to betray his trust. I'm just—" She exhaled and shook her head.

There was no other way to do this, but reach for straightforward honesty. "You've obviously been thinking that my being here, this whole setup, is two miles north of strange?''

"It's not my business to intrude on Mr. Drury's business or social preoccupations."

"We're *not* having an affair."

"Thank you for sharing that. Are congratulations or sympathies in order?"

"I'm not sure. That's what I wanted to talk to you about."

"*Me?* To be perfectly frank, I'd much prefer discussing the merits of yogurt over sour cream."

Rocky leaned across the counter. "Help me! I don't know who else to turn to, and I'm out of my depth with the man."

That stopped his fidgeting. "Most everyone is. He's very strong and knows his own mind. I've never met anyone more in balance with himself. If there's ever been a person you could call self-reliant, it's Mr. Drury."

That's what she hadn't wanted put into words. Of all the men in the world she could be attracted to, falling for, it had to be someone who didn't want to be loved. But she was also beginning to realize that sometimes the bottom line was out of everyone's hands.

"I need to understand what else drives him," she said, trying to entreat McGuire's support. "Does he have dreams that you know about? What pleases him? Have you noticed that he rarely smiles, and even then it's constructed? Criminy H. Columbus, McGuire, a man on top of the world like he is should be happier! So why haven't we heard him break out in a real belly laugh or do anything totally spontaneous?"

"Well, once he did give me half a Monday off when he decided to drive Miss—to the, ah . . . never mind."

Rocky let the subject pass, as well. She didn't want to know about the women who'd been in Worth's life. Especially if her name was Erica. But McGuire's response did tell her something important about him.

Giving a servant a few hours off did not qualify as spontaneous. In other words, Worth was more trapped in his singular, ingrained life-style than she'd suspected. That made her a fool for letting her physical attraction to him get to even this point. She needed to fight it harder, as he was doing, and the easiest way to do that was to keep her focus on her studies and her volunteer work at the youth hostel.

"I just remembered something I needed to research before my next class," she murmured to McGuire.

He looked a bit surprised but mostly relieved to have the conversation veering away from Worth. "I'll give you a ride to the library."

"Um . . . no, thanks. I'll catch the bus over."

Minutes later as she let herself out of the house and headed for the bus stop that would take her in an entirely different direction than the campus, Rocky thought that at least Father Carmichael would be pleased.

As a result of her own considerable progress, he'd suggested that she start a remedial reading program at the hostel. To pass on her skills as she polished them, he'd said.

At first she'd thought it best to beg off. She was already taking a risk with the several hours she spent there a week. As part of their agreement, Worth had made it clear he wasn't encouraging outside interests beyond her schooling. He'd warned her how easy it would be to slip so far behind in her studies that catching up would be impossible.

But under the circumstances she needed this trip. It would keep her mind off *him*. Right now that was worth almost any price.

Six

"**W**here the hell have you been? I was about to phone the police."

Worth watched Roxanne whirl around at the foot of the stairs and stare at him across the space of the foyer as though he were a ghost—or worse. Too experienced in reading guilt in a woman's face, he recognized it in hers an instant before she hid it with a smile.

"You're home early. Or am I late?" The smile wavered. "Um...what's up? Are you coming down with something?"

He did feel ill, but not because he was catching the flu or anything. At least not unless worry and suspiciousness could be classified as a virus. "Let's focus on one set of questions at a time, shall we?"

He meant to sound cool, even arrogant. Damn it, he'd been waiting for hours. He'd come home early to surprise her with another treat outing. They were to go to dinner and then a play. As a reward for her hard work and diligence, he'd told himself. Completely familiar with her schedule, he knew she should have been home three hours ago. Instead, he'd been driving himself crazy wondering if she'd been in an accident, mugged or heaven knew what. As far as he was concerned, he had every right to be upset.

But watching her cross the hardwood floor, hugging books and notebooks to her chest, Worth also felt the resurgence of the same sexual craving that had—despite both of their efforts to fight it—only intensified. As it threatened to override the doubts in his mind, he brutally told himself that it was simply the hint of spring in the air. But he had little success. He was becoming increasingly, totally obsessed with her, and she was playing games with him . . . or betraying him. He could feel it.

"I've been . . . at school," she said, her own gaze moving swiftly over his face as though she hoped to read there how much trouble she was in.

He studied her and acknowledged her loveliness, hurt. Beneath her unzipped white ski jacket—another indulgence he hadn't been able to resist giving her—the black-and-red jumpsuit emphasized her long legs and trim hips. It had been among the first things he'd picked for her. Now he wished he'd chosen something less striking, or that he could hide her in the rags he'd first found her in.

"No, you weren't," he replied, curling his hands into fists. He hated lies most of all. W.H. had tried to convince him that in business essentially everyone lied, but Worth detested deception even there. "It's Friday. Your last class ended at three today."

"True. I meant the library."

"You don't usually stay this late."

"Not when I'm alone, no."

Aha, he thought, although he felt as if the room was closing in on them. "You were with someone?"

"I met a classmate. We studied together and then . . . we went to the campus café for coffee."

It was an innocent enough explanation, and yet Worth could feel the hot coals of possessiveness burn into his belly. "I had plans. For us."

"I'm sorry. If you'd told me earlier . . ."

"Then it wouldn't have been a surprise."

He'd decided she deserved a break, not to mention a reward, for all her hard work. He knew he'd been demanding a great deal from her lately. No matter how hard she'd been striving to please him, he'd been keeping his praise to a minimum, usually focusing only on any weakness he could find in her performance. Not because he didn't see how well she was doing, but because he was trying not to think about her as a woman and how every day he woke to the knowledge that he wanted her more.

Explaining what he'd planned, he said, "It's too late for dinner, but I suppose we could still make the theater in time . . . that is, if you care to go?"

"It'll only take me a few minutes to get ready," she replied, looking more eager to escape than excited.

As good as her word, she returned in only minutes looking demure in a fox gray suit with pearl buttons. Trapped inside his own doubts and unable to express how lovely she looked, Worth simply escorted her to his car.

They had a terrible time. The play, despite rave reviews, proved a disappointment. The intermission deserved four stars for the careful editing that kept conversation to a minimum. They sounded, Worth thought, as they finally settled back in the car, like an old married couple who'd grown to know each other too well.

"Are you hungry?"

"Not really. But if you are . . ."

"No."

He started the car and headed for home. Two blocks of silence, he couldn't contain his curiosity any longer. "So, this classmate of yours . . . is he a local boy?"

"I don't recall saying he was a 'boy.'"

"Well, I'm asking. Is he?"

"Isn't it conceivable that it would be someone of the female persuasion?"

"Yes, but unlikely, considering that you didn't offer the information in the first place."

"Well, maybe I didn't for the simple reason that I don't like being made to feel as though I'm committing a federal offense if I choose to speak with anyone besides *you.*"

His spine should have snapped under the pressure of his tension. "Now I'm your jailer?"

Her silence was damning.

"I see." Indignation burned through his hurt. "Perhaps I am strict, but it's merely a result of being aware of all the pitfalls that could interfere with your studying. Naturally, if you're so unhappy with your life, perhaps you should reconsider our arrangement."

"Maybe I should."

Of course, she didn't. And Worth didn't broach the subject again. In the week that followed, however, he found a multitude of reasons to be home as much as he could. But he soon learned how that gave him too many opportunities to see the comfortable relationship she'd developed with McGuire.

"Did you *really* get kicked out of Buckingham Palace?" he overheard her ask one day, as he paused outside the kitchen. He'd been drawn there by her laughter.

To his amazement McGuire had burst into giggles like a schoolboy. Then his butler told her the story about getting caught carving a too-realistic likeness of the royal profile into the breakfast butter.

It had been a funny story. But envy kept Worth from enjoying it. Pride kept him from joining them, and he withdrew to his study.

After that lessons grew more strained.

"Please don't use that form of the word."

"What?" Roxanne asked, looking up from the passage of the newspaper she'd been reading to him.

"*Height.* To add a *th* sound at the end is a Middle English enunciation and no longer popular."

"That's how the evening news anchor on TV says it."

"Contrary to what you might think, that small device in his ear is not a direct telephone line to Daniel Webster."

"What a relief to know that you're here to set us all straight."

Worth slipped off his own reading glasses and closed the portfolio he'd been trying to look interested in. "You're in a strident mood."

"It's the influence of the company."

"Are you suggesting I'm being unfair?"

"Would it do any good? Chase says you were a tough number as a kid, but this—"

"When did you talk with my brother?"

"We...we had lunch. The other day." She straightened in her seat and met his gaze with determination. "He's fun, Worth."

And you're not. He didn't have to hear the words to know they existed between them. Wanting to crush something between his hands, he placed them flat on the desk blotter. "What matters is that you didn't intend to tell me." When her silence spoke for her, he added, "Why?"

"It didn't concern you." Returning her focus to the paper she cried with forced cheerfulness, "This will improve your mood, Worth—an editorial from some economist anticipating the next financial collapse."

On the following Saturday Worth returned home earlier than anticipated from a golf game. His partner had come down with a mild case of food poisoning, and he didn't have any interest in playing on without him.

As he climbed the stairs and approached his room, Rocky's door swung open. One glance at her red V-necked sweater and black slacks, the look of surprise and unease on her face and he knew he'd caught her on her way out.

"Going somewhere?"

"Ah...just for a walk. Aren't you supposed to be playing golf?"

He told her what had happened, then noted, "Is something wrong? You seem in an awful hurry."

"Only because it's a glorious afternoon. I don't want to waste it."

"Have you finished with your class assignments?"

"Worth, it's Saturday. Aren't I allowed any time to just be *me*?"

No, he thought, his gaze restless as it moved over her face. Because she was the one who was consuming his thoughts both day and night. She was the one driving him mad.

Her color deepened, and as though she could read his mind, she whispered, "You have to stop this. I can't take much more."

"*You* can't?"

"You're treating me like some hothouse flower. Worse—a creature on a leash!"

"Try acting like an adult and I'll stop!"

Her eyes flashed blue fire. "I'm going to St. Timothy's. Not for a walk. To see my friends and people who need me."

Friends. What friends? Where were her friends when she'd almost been raped?

He'd told her back in the beginning that he didn't want her returning to that part of town alone. If visions of what had almost happened there still bothered him, why didn't they haunt her? What's more, he didn't understand why she couldn't put the hostel behind her, too. All those homeless, troubled, undereducated young people—she didn't need the stress, let alone the influence. He'd even sent a sizable check in an effort to ease her conscience.

With a sigh of exasperation she cried, "I'm sharing what I'm learning in a remedial reading class for the kids in the hostel. There...now you know my big dark secret!"

All he knew was this wasn't a one-time spontaneous visit as he'd hoped. "How often?" he asked quietly.

"What difference does it make?" she countered. "They need the help badly, and that's all that should matter. Besides, it's the one place I can go where I don't have to watch every word I say or worry about how I sit or eat. And you know what, Worth? They think I'm pretty wonderful, whether I make a mistake or not.

"I can't please you," she continued, her eyes filling with angry tears. "You go out of your way to find fault with everything I do. You're always so cold to me."

"And you're sarcastic to me."

"You *know* why. I hate seeing how you look at me and then punish me because you don't want to feel what you do."

"That's not up for discussion, Roxanne."

"Right. How foolish of me to even think it would be. Excuse me, I'll miss my bus."

She tried to slip by him. He grabbed her arm, knowing he would have stood in front of a speeding cab if that's what it would take to stop her. But what he didn't count on was her instant retaliation, a furious jerk that momentarily won her freedom.

She got halfway to the stairs before he caught up with her, and with a ruthless tug, pulled her against him. "Damn you . . ."

"Let me go."

"Never."

Because he knew he'd spoken the truth and didn't want to think about what it actually meant, he silenced her with a kiss. Quickly. Yielding to a mindless surge of raw energy, he took her mouth with his, shattering the careful barriers he'd constructed. His defenses were blown away like a hurricane shredding a straw house. All he knew was the painful, blinding need to have her. Now. Before he lost his mind completely.

At first she fought him, trying to elude his kisses and push him away. But she was no match against his greater strength, once he trapped her arms between them. Nevertheless, when he raced his mouth down the side of her neck, she attempted to use the opportunity to reason with him.

"Worth, don't. I can't bear any more of this pushing and pulling."

"No. Neither of us can."

He captured her mouth again, kissing her until she stopped struggling. Slowly her fingers uncurled, trembled against his chest. Then she slid her arms around his neck and clung to him.

Worth reveled in the pleasure of it. The heat of her passion scorched him, just as their bickering these past weeks had debilitated him. But even that wasn't enough.

"I want you, Roxanne," Worth rasped, his body throbbing.

She drew back and stared at him for a moment before she took his head in her hands. "Say that again."

"I want you. Are you going to tell me that's not what you want, too?"

"No. But I do have one—" she paused as though searching for the word "—stipulation."

Now it comes, he thought, keeping his control carefully tethered, the negotiating in the oldest game known between man and woman. "What?" he demanded flatly, trying to ignore the fierce beating of his heart. And the knowledge that he would be willing to pay any price.

"Stop calling me Roxanne."

He didn't know how to respond.

"I'm Rocky. I want you to call me Rocky."

He felt a rush of shame for having thought the worst. "That's all?" he asked, genuinely perplexed.

"It's a lot to me. It's who I am. And I don't think I can survive you very well without its protection."

How easily the tension washed from him. He relaxed, reached up and stroked her cheek. "Knowing this was your first time, you think I'd be anything less than gentle?"

"I want your passion," she replied, leaning into his hand. "But I need my identity. Say it, Worth."

He wondered what her reaction would be if he told her he would get on his knees if that's what it took. "I want you...Rocky."

"Then make love to me," she murmured, once again slipping her arms around his neck.

* * *

She'd never been more sure of a decision in her life. As Worth lifted her into his arms, Rocky's heart overflowed with happiness, and a rush of heady pleasure seeped through every inch of her body. There wasn't another man on earth with whom she wanted to share this moment. Knowing the truth of that made giving herself to him very easy. No matter what happened afterward, she would hold the magic of this afternoon precious and dear for the rest of her life.

He made her feel like a fairy-tale princess, she mused, as he continued the romantic gesture by carrying her into her room. So bright were their surroundings, it made her feel as though they were stepping up to the sun. The ivory walls and the pale yellow draperies and linens blended to create a blinding light. There would be no hiding or pretending here, she realized, as he shut the door behind them. But the thought of such honesty didn't intimidate her. She wanted Worth to see her, all of her... just as she couldn't wait to see him.

He laid her diagonally across the bed. After shrugging out of his suit jacket and tugging off his tie, he stretched alongside her, letting her get used to the feel of his long length pressing against her.

Somehow it was very different from when they were dancing, she thought, as he slid one hand into her hair and sought her lips for a slow, deep kiss. That, too, became all the more intimate in this position. But Rocky knew no fear. Rather, she felt his power radiate through her, buoying up her own strength and confidence. Soon, as it had before, passion rose to a steaming level, and there was only the urgency to explore all of it.

"Tell me if I go too fast," he murmured, his lips grazing her cheek on their journey to explore the length of her throat. "Tell me if anything embarrasses you."

Her heart wrenched with a need to protect him from himself. "You're not going to embarrass me."

He lifted his head and gazed intently into her eyes. "You don't know what I want from you."

Although his expression was fierce and his tone held a warning, she didn't hesitate. "It doesn't matter. When you look at me like that, all I feel is heat, and the worst ache to have you touch me . . . kiss me."

"Like this?" He let his hand graze her cheek again, brushed his thumb across her sensitized lower lip, down the length of her throat . . . to her left breast. In spite of her thick sweater, she could feel her body's instant reaction.

Rocky sucked in a necessary breath and arched to intensify the gentle pressure. "Yes."

"The night I saw you in my tub, it was all I could do not to strip and join you in there."

She loved his gruff tone and smiled at the reluctance with which he spoke. "I was afraid of you then."

"But not now?"

"Now all I know is that if you stop doing that, I'll die."

He was alternately stroking the outer curve of her breast and sweeping his thumb over her nipple. It seemed almost indecent what that subtle caress did to her body and made her wonder if she could survive the pleasure of what would follow.

"I ought to strangle you for trying to leave the house without wearing a bra under this."

But despite the growl he hadn't stopped the seductive things he was doing to her. Rocky purred with contentment. "I hate bras. If you had to wear one, you would, too. I much prefer the feel of silk against my skin. I've imagined . . . is that what a mouth would feel like?''

"There's no comparison," Worth replied with a knowing smile. "My mouth will feel much better."

Before she knew it, he had her out of her sweater. His skillful efficiency forced her to note, "You're very good at this."

"Not as good as you are at tormenting me." It was a flippant remark, but as soon as he spoke, Worth sighed. "I warned you that I would be vastly more experienced than you. Is it finally registering, Rocky? Do you want to change your mind?"

Shaking her head, she took his hand and placed it back where her red camisole peaked. "I like that one of us knows what to do. Teach me everything."

Uttering a soft oath, his big hand covering her completely, Worth kissed her again. The silk trapped between them heated, creating a delicious, velvety sensation with every shift of his fingers. Rocky thought she might be turning completely wanton, but she couldn't keep from writhing against him in her attempt to get closer. Worth, however, seemed to approve, finally helping her by rolling onto his back and dragging her completely over his body for a breathtaking new intimacy.

Beneath the canopy of her hair, her camisole straps slipped off her shoulders, and silk melted away exposing her. With a groan Worth raised his head and took her into his mouth.

Rocky gasped as pleasure, sharp and fast, shot through her body. Instinctively she shifted to clasp his head to her, while the lower half of her body sought a more perfect closeness with his.

A brief tremor shook Worth. "Sweet hell," he whispered against her dampened skin. "Do that again."

She did, crying out when he mimicked the motion by sweeping his tongue over her.

"Again."

She complied to his rasped entreaty and felt herself grow hotter and moist where his aroused body burned into hers. But it still wasn't enough.

Worth seemed to agree, because a moment later he whipped the camisole off her and rolled her back beneath him. Breathless and slightly dizzy, Rocky laughed and brushed her hair out of her eyes. Then she began unbuttoning his shirt. Or tried to. What brought her up short was Worth's determination to repeat his earlier caresses to her right breast.

She gripped his shoulders as a new wave of pleasure threatened to sweep her away. "Oh . . . please."

"That's my plan, little one."

"No, I mean it's . . ."

"Too much?"

"So good. Worth, let me make you feel like this."

He sat up and tugged her astride his lap. "In case you haven't noticed, you already are. Almost too much." But he let her unbutton his shirt, helped her remove it and then waited patiently as she stared.

Were men supposed to be this beautiful? she wondered, desire churning within her. He was. She had always been aware of his size and strength, but as she ran her hands over his broad chest and combed her fingers through the triangular mat of black hair, she gained a new appreciation for his physical perfection.

"Go ahead," Worth said, his voice somewhat strained. "Do whatever you want."

Encouraged, she leaned forward and let her hair sweep across his chest, the ends flicking over her legs and his. At the sound of an involuntary groan, she smiled and added her hands and finally the intimacy of her mouth.

Barely allowing her to begin to satisfy her curiosity about him, Worth filled his hands with her hair and forced her head up, muttering, "You're too good a student," before locking his mouth to hers.

This time their kiss was less tame, more demanding. Worth also shifted his hold. He slid his hands to her hips and clasped her more firmly against his aroused body. The rhythmic plumbing of his tongue in and out of her mouth matched the erotic rise and fall of his hips against hers.

"This is what it's going to feel like when I'm inside you," he whispered against her mouth. "Only better."

"Soon," she moaned, convinced it couldn't possibly get any better.

"No." He licked the moisture from her lips and eased her back onto the bed. "Not yet. We don't want to rush this time. It's precious...something to be remembered with pleasure. Always."

Gentle now, he trailed kisses down her body to the waistband of her slacks. Just as carefully, he unbuttoned them and lowered the zipper. If his previous caresses had propelled her sensory education to new realms, he now rocketed them to the exhilarating unknown by pressing his open mouth over the lace panel of her panties.

She dug her short nails into the taut muscles of his back. "Worth!"

Although he didn't reply, he surprised her again as he began to lower her slacks...only her slacks. She wanted to kiss him for his sensitivity. No matter how sure she was about wanting this, no matter how confident she felt that he truly wanted her, she appreciated this extra time to regain her self-confidence about exposing herself in this relentless light.

He made it so easy. By the time he finished removing her jogging shoes and socks along with the slacks, she was eager to scramble to her knees again, eager to do the same for him.

"You amaze me," he murmured, brushing her hair behind one shoulder.

"Maybe not for long," she said, grimacing at her clumsiness as she fumbled with his belt buckle. "The mechanics get complicated when you're sitting."

"They get even more complicated when a man's aroused," Worth replied, standing. Slipping out of his shoes, he finished loosening his belt and unzipped his pants. Then, without hesitation, he pushed off the rest of his clothes. "Still feeling brave?"

Rocky reached out, her hand poised to touch but hesitant. Awed. "Worth...I don't have words."

"I do. It pleases me very much to know you want me," he said, as he bent to lightly bite at her lower lip. "Because I want *you* to enjoy every moment as fully as I plan to."

As he reached behind her and ripped the bedspread back off the pillows, she wondered at his control. All she could think of was the joy she felt at being desired by this incredible man. "I'm sorry, I should be helping—"

"Shh." As she attempted to assist him, he caught her around the waist and planted another kiss on her shoulder. "This isn't very spontaneous, I know. But with it being your first time, I don't want you to be upset if you find yourself..."

"Bleeding?"

He disappeared into the bathroom, returning quickly with a large green towel, which he spread across the bed. "Does that worry you?"

"No." Because she raced around at breakneck speed, she was forever bumping into corners or scratching herself at some job or another. A little blood didn't upset her, nor pain. What would bother her would be never knowing the pleasure this man could bring her.

But there was something she knew she had to consider. "I suppose I should ask about..."

"Protection?" Worth reached over to the foot of the bed for his suit jacket and drew out his billfold. From inside he took a small foil packet that he tossed onto one of the pillows. "Now," he murmured, his attention completely returning to her, "let's concentrate on that spontaneity again."

Oh, he was very good, she thought, as he kissed her backward until she lay across the towel. But she believed in this exhibition of sincerity, and it melted her heart as nothing had for weeks, months.

When he bent low to capture her mouth with his, she wrapped her arms around his neck and drew him closer. With a groan he relented and let her feel the full length of him, his naked power and strength. It was the most stunning, enervating feeling she'd ever experienced.

Within seconds the wildfire reignited between them. Worth answered her bold entreaty with his own hungry assault, his hands skillful as they scorched a trail down her back to slide into her panties and cup her bottom. Hunger gripped Rocky deep in her womb and she whimpered her need, wishing the last scrap of material separating them would already be gone.

As though he read her mind, Worth traced another series of kisses along her body. When he reached her hips, his fingers tightened, relaying his own desire.

"Help me," she breathed.

Wordlessly he drew that last bit of clothing down her legs and let them join the other castaways scattered on the floor. Then he drew his fingers back up the length of her legs, his touch so light tears unexpectedly filled her eyes. But what she wasn't prepared for was the brush of his lips against her inner knee, the lover's nip on her inner thigh . . . and then his hot breath at the center of her heat.

"Don't say no."

She couldn't have said anything if she'd wanted to. As he touched her, she sucked in a sharp breath to try, but it swelled in her throat blocked by the cry of ecstasy that rose from her soul.

"Just feel," he crooned. "So beautiful...so sweet...just flow with the pleasure."

What followed was as blinding as the light filling the room, as deafening as a tidal wave crashing over her, as overwhelming as if that same wave was racing her to some pinnacle and then dragging her back. Rocky took the entire journey, her senses humming from all the emotions she experienced. At her first peak she bit back a cry, at her second, Worth left her momentarily, only to return and begin finding his place inside her before she began the descent.

Eager for his nearness, fearless against any pain that might be involved with taking him inside her, she wrapped her legs around him and buried her face in the curve of his shoulder. Yes, he filled her to a bursting point; but he was so powerful and throbbing with life, he reignited her desire until she trembled with it.

"Does it hurt?" he rasped.

"No. It's incredible. I can feel your heartbeat inside me."

He sucked in a sharp breath. "This is not a good time to be provocative. I should warn you I'm very close."

Rocky slid her hands to his bottom as he'd done to her. She loved that he was taut even there. "Tell me what to do to please you. I want to make you feel everything I am."

Worth raised himself on his elbows, and for the first time she saw the strain working on his face. "Just hold me, and don't..."

"What?" She felt somehow what he held back might be most important. "What, Worth?"

"Don't stop wanting me."

Burying his face in her hair, he swore and thrust deep into her. Once. Then again. And suddenly, shuddering with his release, he crushed her close and whispered her name again and again, spawning her own new spasms of ecstasy.

Worth shut his eyes against the glare of the sun and the reality staring him in his face. But it didn't help, nor did lowering his head to the dark softness of Rocky's hair. Nothing would wipe the truth away, just as this one stolen hour wouldn't quench his desire for the small woman in his arms.

Rocky. How quickly he'd adapted to even thinking of her that way. She'd bewitched him. Or he'd become obsessed with her. In any case he was in serious danger of losing the strict control he'd always kept of his life... his emotions.

Could this be love?

He didn't like the feeling at all. What sane person would? He felt like a mass of gelatin teetering on the peak of K2 in the midst of hurricane force winds. His insides felt queasy, and there wasn't enough oxygen in the room. And yet... he knew if he opened his eyes and looked at her lovely, lovely face, his heart would ache anew with longing for her.

It wasn't a reassuring feeling.

"In the movies this is where the hero gets dressed and tells the gullible heroine that he has to leave for no-man's-land or some deadly mission," Rocky said, her voice sounding very young and painfully hesitant. "He manages some competent speech about how special she is, but that he's the wrong guy for her and to try to forget him."

"I'm not hero material."

"Oh, I don't know. It takes a rare man to take a complete stranger into his home. To risk his own life to save hers. To—"

"Don't." Worth grimaced at the pretty pictures she insisted on painting of him. "I may not always be a complete bastard, but I'm a selfish one. I've just proven it by taking advantage of you, of your vulnerability to me. Why aren't you noticing that?"

"Because this was my choice. No matter how much you keep trying to see me as a young innocent, Worth, I'm a woman with a mind of her own. I make my own decisions, and it was *my* decision to give myself to you. The only blame you can take on is for being so devastatingly handsome and sexy that I couldn't resist wanting you."

Worth rose on his elbow and leaned over her. He smoothed a hand over her hair, frustrated, and extremely hungry to taste her sweet mouth again. "You're a fool. An exquisite, desirable little fool. If you had an ounce of sense, you'd tell me to keep my hands off you."

"I'd rather ask you to make love to me again."

"Rocky..." Unable to resist, Worth bent to kiss her forehead. Then her cheek, her chin. He couldn't seem to stop. "Rocky..."

"It's all right," she whispered, running her hands down his back. "I'm not going to complicate your life."

He would have laughed if he wasn't feeling so troubled. Complicate his life? She was tying him up in knots. And yet, he could no more make himself leave her alone than he could regret what had just happened between them.

"Rocky," he said urgently, before he could think of another reason to keep silent, "I want us to... Don't lock me out of your room or your bed."

"You mean you want us to be lovers?"

The term bothered him. Granted, it filled his mind with erotic images of them tangled in heated passion, but it also sounded so... temporary. "For as long as we're together. Will you give me your body as willingly as you've given me your mind?"

Seven

"Don't tell me you said yes?"

After the shock wore off, Rocky had to fight back hysterical laughter. The way she figured it, one impetuous outburst was already pushing it when one was in a confessional.

"Father C, you're supposed to fine me, not editorialize," she whispered through the heavy screen. "Jeez, this is embarrassing. If I'd known it was you in here this afternoon, and not half-deaf Father Bascone, I'd have fine-tuned my confession to a couple curses and stuff. I would never have admitted that I'd been having an affair with Worth for the past two months."

A soft keening sound drifted over from his side of the screen and then the priest whispered back, "Don't *say* such things to me, Rocky. Premeditation is a sin, too."

"Hey, we're supposed to be honest in here, right? You can't have it both ways."

He sighed heavily. "I've failed you. As soon as I heard you'd moved away from the neighborhood and into that man's house, I should have recognized his intentions weren't pure."

"You can't be blamed, Father. That check he sent for the hostel would have fooled any bloodhound."

"Thank you for your generous spirit, my child. Now I only feel like a moral mercenary."

This time Rocky did indulge in a low chuckle. "Let's get out of the hot box and talk, Father C. I figure God can hear us in the sunlight as good as He can here, don't you?"

A few minutes later Rocky met the priest in the garden between the church, his living quarters and the hostel. The early May sun was edging toward the roof of the parsonage, and Rocky patted the iron bench by a bed of pansies, urging Father Carmichael to join her.

He did, but he kept his gaze averted. Finally, focusing on his hands clasped tight between his spread knees, he said, "I wish you weren't so cheerful about this."

"Why?" She laughed. "I'm happy."

"For how long?"

"I don't know. Who knows how long anything lasts? Is that the point? Longevity? I know a couple of people who've been married thirty, forty, fifty years, Father C, and they're miserable as heck. In the summer when I used to walk down the alley, there wasn't a day I didn't hear yelling and screaming coming down from their opened apartment windows."

"The key word there is *married,* Rocky. At least the couples you mentioned aren't living in sin."

"Maybe they got that rule right, but they broke all the others. That's a bit hypocritical for my tastes." Rocky shifted to face her glum-faced friend. "Worth's good to me, and gentle. He cares for me."

"Not enough to make an honest woman of you."

Because she knew that secretly she would rather be a bride than a mistress, Rocky didn't attempt to argue that point. But she wanted Father Carmichael to see why she'd made the decision she did. "He isn't very good with personal relationships."

"That's not an acceptable excuse."

"I'm not excusing him, I'm explaining him to you." She spread her hands in a gesture of helplessness. "One thing I'm learning as I live in his world is that there needs to be a line, some point where you have to stop trying to make people into what you think they should be and accept them for who they are. It's much easier to see in his environment of glitz and glamour and wheeling and dealing, because everything is bigger than life. It's been an eye-opener to discover that people like Worth may be risk takers with their money, but not their hearts. Right now, all that he can give me of himself, he is. And it's pretty wonderful."

Father Carmichael reached over and took one of her hands between his. "And what if that's all he can ever give you?"

The thought had crossed her mind—for about ten seconds. Then Rocky had thrust it into the farthest reaches of her mind for sanity's sake. Because she couldn't let herself linger on such a frightening concept.

"I'm not pretending to have all the answers, Father. And I refuse to ask myself to live that far in the future. The important thing is to make the most of today and not waste it." A movement out of the corner of her eye caught Rocky's attention. Glancing over she saw a redhead walking into the hostel. "Speaking of which, there's Dani. I want to talk to her about Eddie. I overheard him telling one of the other kids that he would try going home again if he thought his older brother would lay off with the beatings. Maybe she can find his brother and talk to him."

"You know if you're not careful, Rocky, Dani's going to find herself with a partner on her hands," Father Carmichael said, his expression softening.

Rocky could feel the blush creep into her cheeks, but it was offset by a warm rush of pleasure. "Well, I could do a lot worse, couldn't I?"

"Who is she?"

After a final glance and wave out the passenger window, Rocky turned to Chase and grinned. "Forget it. Back there's no-man's-land."

"The church?"

"No, Dani. Danielle Lanier."

"Nice. Classy-looking redhead."

"Too nice and too classy for you."

"Ouch. I thought we'd become friends?"

"We have," Rocky assured him, securing her seat belt. "But Dani's entire life is focused on Heaven Can Wait, the organization for runaways, drop-outs and all the rest of life's misfits. And it's more than your usual commitment. She lost her twin tragically, a former priest at St. Timothy's. Father Daniel was shot by a kid who thought he was a cop busting him on his first drug sale."

"Tough break. I still intend to meet her, though."

"Intend. Jeez, you Drury men are pushy."

"Maybe, but unlike my brother, at least I allow you to make your own mistakes."

Rocky knew he'd made his point with that one. In the two months since she and Worth had become lovers, Chase had stood by, watching in concern, although he'd hid it well with humor.

"Okay, okay, I'll think about it." Knowing how stubborn he had to be to grow up so different from his brother and father, she decided all she could do right now was to change the subject. "I appreciate the ride. What brought you to this side of town?"

"The company's considering taking on a new project and I volunteered to inspect the place."

"That was risky to do alone."

"I called in a favor from a cop I know. It went okay."

Why did she get the feeling there was more to Chase than met the eye? She shook her head. "You Drurys," she murmured again.

"Speaking of which, does my brother know you're here?"

"No. I'm sure he thinks I'm in class. But the instructor canceled due to a family emergency."

"Guess I'm not the only one who enjoys to live life closer to the edge."

Rocky gave him a half shrug, unwilling to see it that way. She knew Worth continued to frown upon her coming to the neighborhood, but their new closeness had given her a way to take his mind off that particular conflict.

"For what it's worth," Chase continued with some reluctance, "he's a different man these days. I know a bunch of people at the office who appreciate that and hope it sticks."

So did she. Worth remained the most complex man she'd ever met. Extremely proud and closed, he still didn't share too much about himself. He was also continuing to be a demanding benefactor and mentor. But when they were together...yes, there was a change.

He couldn't seem to keep from touching her. Physical contact was like oxygen to him, and it certainly had its effect on her. A light touch at the back of her neck when he passed her could ruin her concentration, the caress of his fingers brushing over her hand in a restaurant would make her senses hum with sexual awareness. Even if she was studying and he was working behind his desk, his gaze had a tendency to stray to her every few minutes, as though he had to make certain she hadn't vanished.

When he yielded to stronger urges, she became strictly a sensual being. A stolen kiss in a dark doorway as they left a theater would have them running like children to the car in order to get home sooner. If he tugged her onto his lap as he took a call, she enjoyed his willingness to let her explore him, until, abruptly, he ended the conversation, swept her into his arms and carried her to her room. She lived for those moments when he let her see the man he hid from the rest of the world—the man she'd fallen head over heels in love with.

"I'm sorry he hasn't gotten to know the side of you that I have, Chase," she said, wanting to reassure her friend.

If there was a social function where all the Drurys made an appearance, Chase always hovered nearby to ensure that she had someone to talk to. Most of all she was grateful that he made a point to offset W.H.'s apathy toward her. Since meeting her, the senior Drury had made it clear that he didn't approve of her presence in his eldest son's life and intended to ignore her in the hopes that she would go away.

Of course, she understood why the social columns labeled Chase a "wicked heartthrob." He adored women, and there didn't seem to be more than two serious bones in his body—at least not that he seemed willing to admit publicly. But Rocky had a feeling Worth's younger brother was a better actor than people recognized, and that like Worth he bore his own wounds and insecurities.

Chase responded with the famous Drury snort. "Just because I'm not the bossy bull stampeding over everything in my path the way W.H. does, or brood and glower like Worth, doesn't mean my life's an ongoing fairy tale."

"But you don't let it show."

He was silent a moment before he admitted, "I guess I have had it a bit easier than Worth. At least I was too young to actually miss our mother as a face or a touch. And for all his tirades, W.H. never pressured me to achieve the way he did Worth."

Glad to have the subject come up, Rocky asked, "Is losing your mother what's made Worth so reluctant to trust?"

"I don't think it's that cut-and-dried. Worth's a mixture of things and all of them are complicated. It goes beyond being the firstborn, the heir to the throne and all that. He was literally weened listening to the morning stock reports out of Tokyo. I can remember us charging downstairs one Christmas morning to find W.H. hanging up from a business call—God only knows whose day he ruined—glare at Worth and growl, 'Never trust anyone, my boy. The moment you do they'll betray you.'"

"That's awful!"

"Depends on how you look at things. Worth may be a miserable failure as a human being, but you can't deny he's a perfected business machine."

Feeling a sudden chill, the kind she'd once heard Badger explain as "a ghost walking over my grave," Rocky rubbed her arms. "He needs more."

Chase beamed with an affectionate smile. "Seems to me he's found it." In the next instant he swore and hit the brakes. "Oh, damn."

"What's wrong?" Rocky followed his gaze.

"Worth's home early. I'd better let you off here."

So he was. Spotting his car, she collected her books and released her seat belt. But she didn't get out, despite Chase pulling up to the curb several houses away.

"No," she said, nodding. "Pull up in front of the house. If Worth sees us together, I've nothing to hide."

Chase stared at her for a moment as though she'd lost her mind, but he eventually succumbed to her stubbornness and eased his car down to the brownstone.

With a quick word of thanks, Rocky jumped out of the car and raced up the sidewalk. It was strange how her nervousness was offset by her excitement to be with him.

She let herself into the house with the key Worth had entrusted to her. McGuire peeked out from the kitchen, his expression changing to an animated look of relief. Then he signaled that Worth was upstairs.

"Is something wrong? Is he sick?" she asked in a loud whisper.

He shrugged. "You're better at reading that stone face than I am. All he said was to take messages on any calls that might come in."

Gripping her books even more tightly, Rocky ignored every lesson in deportment she'd learned these past months and took the stairs two at a time. Worth hadn't beaten her home since the day they'd had that terrible argument. Were they about to have another? Had she forgotten some function he'd wanted her to attend with him? Had he seen her with Chase and read it wrong?

His bedroom door was shut. A good sign? Her mind racing, she rushed into her room, threw her books on a nearby chair and froze.

There on the bed lay a pink, long-stemmed rose.

Mesmerized, she crossed over to it. Enchanted, she hesitated in picking it up. Not only was it perfect, each petal a breathtaking specimen with its own intoxicating scent, but the surprise of it put her off balance.

Touched by this latest display of romance, Rocky spun around, intent on rushing across the hall—and found Worth watching her from behind the door. "Oh, you sneak!" she cried, running to him.

Launching herself into his arms, she cut off his laugh by pressing her mouth to his. Within seconds he took control and turned an eager kiss into one of somber exploration.

Only the need to breathe made her pull away. "What are you doing home? What brought all this on?" she asked, breathless.

"Necessity. I was on the phone, deep in a conversation with my third irascible client of the afternoon, and I realized I was tired of beating my head against a wall. I thought I could come home and at least look at a beautiful woman while taking this abuse."

"Thanks a lot!"

With a throaty laugh, he nipped at her ear. "Now do you want to hear the real reason?"

"Only if you keep in the part about me being beautiful."

"Consider it done." Worth lifted her completely into his arms and began carrying her to his room. "I was looking out my office window and saw the flower vendor way down below on the sidewalk. When I saw that pink rose, all I could think was that it reminded me of your skin, especially when you're soaking in my tub. I had the strongest urge to see you that way again."

Through his bedroom he strode. But he didn't stop there. When he headed toward his bathroom, Rocky said warily, "Worth, what are you up to? You wouldn't!"

Even as he smiled, she told herself he wasn't the sort to do more than one impulsive thing in one day. Then he stepped out of his shoes.

She hastily kicked off her jogging shoes and tightened her grip around his neck. "I'm not sure what bubble bath would do to my jeans and sweater, but you're going to ruin your suit—*pants!*" she gasped, as he stepped with her into the sunken tub. "Oh, Worth, I don't believe you're doing this."

"Why not?"

He lowered them into the water in slow motion. As bubbles rose around her shoulders and steaming water seeped through her clothes, weighing down her hair, Rocky sucked in a long breath. "Because this is so...so..."

"Spontaneous?"

"Wild," she said, barely able to get the words out. Concerned to save her flower, she spotted the uncorked bottle of champagne on the side of the tub and stuffed it inside.

"Hey!"

"Hey yourself," she murmured, rewrapping her arms around his neck and kissing him with the full joy she was feeling. She didn't need bubbling wine to coax her into the right mood. She didn't need any more words or gestures. That Worth had done something so out of character, so delightful, stole her heart completely.

"Help me get you out of this," he muttered, restlessly grappling with the expanding mass of her tunic-style sweater.

Because of the added weight of her hair, it became a complicated procedure. "Wait." Feeling as though she'd already drunk her fill of wine, Rocky fumbled with the buttons at the front of her sweater and then shrugged out of the widened collar. Then she rose to her knees and it plopped down her arms and into the tub.

As she laughed, Worth swore and wiped soap from his face. But his discomfort didn't stop him for long; she barely had her jeans unfastened when he leaned forward and, framing her breasts with his hands, buried his face between them. The wet silk of her white camisole created a delicious layer of warmth against her skin. The added heat and sensitivity of Worth's hands coaxed her eyelids to drift shut as she basked in the heady sensuality of the moment.

When she shifted her hands to cup the back of his head, he groaned. "This is what I wanted. Your vibrance... your sweet acceptance." Turning his head, he nuzzled her left breast. "Let me pour us some wine, sweetheart, and we'll enjoy this slowly."

"None for me." Already feeling drunk from the passion he spawned in her, she again sank down onto his lap and began peeling out of her camisole, as well. That was all she needed, wanted, the freedom to feel. Him.

"Maybe you're right," he murmured, his gaze dropping to the exposed swell of her breasts. He helped her lift the camisole over her head, then it, too, sank beneath the froth in the tub. "I'd rather taste you."

His big hands grasped her by the waist, and he lifted her to eye level again. She smiled, loving his controlled strength and the passion smoldering in his eyes. Within seconds, however, the sweet mood was replaced by something less tame, and she dug her fingers into his shoulders as Worth avidly explored her from breast to waist like a starving man.

She arched backward, following the pull from the weight of her hair. Shifting one arm around her waist, Worth used his right hand to unfasten her slacks. Then he began pushing the rest of her clothes into the water.

Anticipation created its own heat and turned the room into a steam bath. Rocky felt it melt her from the outside in, just as rapidly as Worth's caresses melted her from the inside out, until, out of necessity, she sought the support of marble to keep her afloat. Worth used the moment to finish stripping the last of her clothes off her.

She'd never felt self-conscious about being nude in front of him, but several weeks of experience as his lover made her enjoy the bubbles that provided a fragile barrier to his restless, probing gaze. It added to her confidence and gave her a sense of allure she might not otherwise have allowed herself to indulge in.

She reached up and scooped her heavy hair off her neck, knowing the gesture lifted her breasts out of the water. Yet the bubbles continued to hide her from Worth's view.

"Sweet heaven," he breathed. "You're so beautiful I ache just looking at you."

Scooping a handful of the fragile prisms from one breast, she raised them mouth-high and blew them gently toward him. Then she sat up and murmured, "I feel the same way when I look at you. Let me help you out of the rest of your things."

She focused on unbuttoning his soaked shirt first. But she soon discovered there was something about wet clothes that complicated the task—especially when Worth provided a wicked torment under the water.

"Problems?" he teased. "Surely you can think of an easier way to do that?"

"You can't be serious," she replied, searching his unwavering gaze. There she found challenge ... and entreaty.

What do you need? she wondered silently.

You. Everything you can give me, he seemed to reply.

Coerced, she gave a swift jerk and tore the shirt wide. Buttons popped and splattered into the water. Although a part of her felt wickedly bold, she also felt a unique tenderness as she created this fantasy he seemed to crave so much.

Together they stripped off the shirt. Rocky explored Worth's powerful chest, splaying her fingers wide and combing them through the mat of sable hair. She found the insistent thrum of his heart. Wanting it to beat even more strongly, she bent to his already hard nipple and stroked him with her tongue.

A husky groan rose from Worth's throat as he leaned backward, taking Rocky with him. Settling against the back of the tub, he drew her against the hard wall of his chest. Even as he sought her mouth, she parted her lips, eager to take him.

Nothing had ever felt this good. Accepting the demanding surge of his tongue, Rocky curled her own around his and eagerly locked her knees around his hips. As she slipped her hand under the water and stroked her fingers against the swollen line of his zipper, he broke their kiss to suck in a quick breath.

"I can't decide what I want more," he rasped, running his hands down her back to press her even closer, "your boldness or your honesty."

"Where you're concerned they're the same thing. Would you think me too pushy if I suggested you're still wearing too many clothes?"

"I'd worry if you didn't."

In their eagerness to get him undressed, they almost went under, allowing another moment of tender laughter. But finally the last of his clothing was gone and so was their lighter mood.

When their bodies, slick with water and desire came together again, Rocky closed her eyes, trembling at the wondrous differences between her body and his. Now was the time to savor.

Worth, too, grew very somber, pressing a kiss to her forehead. "You make me ache."

"Me, too."

"I don't want to prolong it any longer. Take me inside you, Rocky. Come to me. Burn for me."

So seduced by the soothing water, stimulated by the kisses and caresses, their joining was smoother than a whisper across satin. Groaning his pleasure, Worth filled his hands with her hair and kissed her as deeply, as thoroughly as he filled her.

Behind closed lids, Rocky watched a canvas of midnight blue fill with swirling stars, converging into a white-hot mass that seemed to pierce straight through to her core. Burning, she met Worth's strong thrust, rocking against him, wanting to reach some pinnacle, some relief from the fever he'd ignited in her.

So good, so good, she thought, spreading kisses over his face. She loved the chiseled planes, the hint of rough whiskers along his jaw, the salty taste as sweat blended with the bathwater. She yearned to hear the harsh sound of his breath, as well. Giving him pleasure meant the world to her. But Worth was nothing if not a fair and thorough lover.

Despite his own craving for satisfaction, he reached down, unerring in his search for the sensitive folds that clasped him to her. With breathtaking skill, he once again showed her how vulnerable she was to his touch.

"Worth..."

"That's it...come closer, sweetheart," he encouraged, as the water lapped around them. "Closer..."

She couldn't get near enough to him, hold him tight enough. But he encouraged her to try, his words bold, his voice turning raw in its intensity.

And then came the wild claiming kiss that dragged the very breath out of her and spawned the explosion of spasms deep within her. Seconds later, Worth shuddered as he reached his own pulsating climax.

It always amazed him how, after making love with Rocky, the strangest emotions tried to inch past the barriers of his mind and nest in his heart. Feelings that made him uneasy, like the urge to protect, vulnerability... and least comfortable of all, need.

As the exquisite woman in his arms bestowed yet another butterfly kiss to the side of his neck, Worth struggled to put reality in perspective. It wasn't easy.

From that first spontaneous afternoon when they'd made love, Rocky had proved a surprise. Brave, sweet, giving. *Trusting*. That, above all, affected his resolve to keep desire separate and apart from the rest of his life.

He couldn't help wanting her, but he knew he had to fight allowing his emotions to go beyond that point. The sum total of all his life experiences demanded it. As much as he enjoyed, craved, her presence in his world, he knew he could be nothing more than an experience for her, a stage in her very young life. Hopefully a positive, memorable one, but a stage nonetheless.

They simply weren't suited for each other, and he wasn't a snob to see that. Yes, she'd come far, working hard to expand her horizons. He didn't tell her often enough how proud he was of her. But the fact remained, they were worlds apart in too many ways not to take notice.

And she deserved better than him.

Yet she gave him something he craved, something he couldn't seem to fill himself with enough. Why else had he rushed home this afternoon to willingly make a fool of himself? Yet, sweet nymph that she was, she hadn't laughed at him, but had joined him in his winsome adventure, responding to his invitation for a late afternoon of illicit love.

God, he didn't want to think about this ending. At the same time, he would be a fool not to remember that theirs was a love affair that ran against a brutally relentless clock. For both their sakes, he had to remember that.

As he sighed inwardly, a wholly different thought struck him. He realized a mistake.

"Thank you."

Despite the shock waves that raced through his mind, Rocky's sweet, husky voice touched his heart, revitalizing a warmth he dreaded losing. Turning his head, he planted a kiss at her temple. But reality kept intruding.

How could he have been so thoughtless? How could he have forgotten to protect her?

Forgot? You?

His conscience was right. To forget was for the innocent . . . and wholly forgivable. What he'd done was to put his own desires first. He had *neglected* to protect her.

Worth swore silently.

"I'm sorry for ruining the champagne," Rocky continued.

"Never mind. I doubt one little flower harmed it." Reaching for the bottle, he held aside the stem and poured some wine into one of the slender tubes of crystal he'd also set out for them. More romantic ridiculousness, he brooded, aware it would take something far more potent for him to escape himself.

Neglected. In his entire life, he'd never been careless with a woman.

Preoccupied, Worth offered Rocky the first sip. Not surprising, she refused, and he gratefully gulped it down. Avoiding her surprised look, he set the glass aside and combed his hair back from his face.

"Worth? What's wrong?" she asked, concern dimming the happiness in her glorious eyes.

"Oh, nothing." He laughed bitterly. "Nothing except that I should be whipped raw."

Clearly, she didn't know what to make of that. "You're the most thoughtful, generous man I've ever met," she began. And leaning forward, she bestowed a kiss on his chin, then another on his left shoulder.

She would have planted a third over his heart, but he quickly reached for a towel and climbed out of the tub. The last thing he needed was to listen to compliments—and for her to feel his heart's erratic pounding.

"Worth . . . ?"

He hated hearing the hurt and confusion in her voice. But what he hated more was having put them both in this position.

"You'll want to dry off before you catch a chill," he said, not quite looking at her.

He felt her gaze. He tried to turn his back to her and knew he couldn't do it. Securing the towel around his waist, he swung around to face her again.

"I didn't protect you," he said.

Realization, then relief registered in her eyes. "I trust you, Worth. You told me yourself that you'd had tests done."

He hadn't even been thinking about *that* problem. "Pregnancy, Rocky. I didn't protect you from an unwanted pregnancy."

That earned him a silent "Oh" from her.

She scooted her legs toward her chest and rested her chin on her knees. Surrounded by bubbles, he thought she resembled a particularly lovely, if suddenly shy mermaid. Desire flared in Worth anew, and for an instant he actually wondered if it would be so bad, wondered how *she* would feel if they'd created a child together.

"You needn't worry," she said softly. "I've been taking care of myself."

He shook his head. This time he was the one who was slow to follow.

"A week after we... after that first time we were together, I made an appointment to see a doctor. She told me that even if you were careful, that... that a little insurance would be wise considering our, um, unique relationship. She gave me a prescription," she explained, as he continued to stare at her.

A prescription. Like the bubbles that were beginning to pop around her, the image of a tiny pink infant nestled against her breast vanished.

Worth felt empty and very foolish.

He didn't notice Rocky rising and getting out of the tub, until she was beside him. She touched his arm.

"Please talk to me."

"Why didn't you tell me?"

"I should have. After all, I paid for the pills and the office visit with the allowance you give me."

"To hell with the money!" Irrationally upset, the last thing he wanted to think about was that. He'd insisted on the allowance—which he knew she hadn't wanted to take— because he hadn't wanted her to try to juggle school *and* a job.

Rocky fell silent a moment. Then she offered, "I was only trying to shoulder my share of responsibility, Worth."

And she was doing so with a great deal more maturity and class than he was. "I'm sorry. I suppose I'm more on edge today than I thought."

"No, I don't think that's all there is to this. Something just happened, and now you're putting up a wall between us."

"I told you this has nothing to do with you."

"And I don't believe you. I think... does it bother you to feel as much as you do when we make love, Worth?"

He'd always known she was bright, but her acuteness now affected him like a blow to his heart. Already turned to retreat to his bedroom, he spun around and faced her. "What?"

Although her composure faltered somewhat, she continued bravely. "I think discovering how good it is between us bothers you. It's something you hadn't counted on. Needing me, I mean."

Hearing his thoughts put into words terrified him. Worth stepped away from them, from her. "I don't *need* people, Roxanne," he said stiffly. "Don't confuse my...wanting you with anything more. I'd hate to see you get hurt."

Eight

———

Rocky handled the blow differently than expected. In the days that followed, Worth kept a close, though discreet, eye on her, and soon found himself surprised. Impressed. She'd worked hard to make it appear as though she'd taken his outburst in stride, seemed content, focused and, as usual, a bit irreverent.

Even so, Worth knew he'd hurt her deeply. Nothing could hide that. The shadow of sorrow in her eyes was as dark now as during the weeks after Badger's death. Nor could he miss noticing how she did everything except lock her door to keep him out of her bed.

The changes were in the forefront of his mind a week later when he arrived home late, knowing he had to change quickly if he was to be on time for the business league's fund-raising banquet—a roast honoring W.H. His dilemma was that he'd asked Rocky to attend with him—

weeks ago. But right now he didn't have a clue as to whether she'd changed her mind or not.

He let himself into the house and headed straight for his study to drop off his briefcase. His glance fell on the stack of mail on his desk. No time for that, he knew. Hearing a sound behind him and hoping it was Rocky, he spun around.

"Good evening, sir. Running a bit late this evening," McGuire said, pausing in the doorway.

Was it his own edginess, or was McGuire taking pains to state the obvious more than usual? "I got tied up in a meeting across town," he replied, glancing through the phone messages beside the mail. Finding none he cared to deal with, he threw the lot of them into the wastepaper basket beneath the desk.

"Is Rocky in yet?" he asked, unable to contain his curiosity any longer. He'd long since given up on trying to get his employee to think of her as Miss Roxanne or Miss Grimes.

"For hours now."

On the heels of a mild relief came confusion. "You mean she came home early from St.—er, whatsis?"

"Timothy's. No, sir. I mean she didn't go at all today."

Hadn't gone to what he humorlessly referred to as her second home? "It's Friday. She's always there Mondays, Wednesdays and Fridays." As a lifetime devotee to routine and a stickler for schedules, Worth knew her weekly commitments as well as he did his own.

"Not today she wasn't."

"Is she ill?"

"Now that you mention it, she did seem on the quiet side. On the other hand, her coloring was up. That could've been from fever, I daresay. But—"

"Never mind." Frustrated, Worth ran a hand over his hair.

"All I know is that she made one telephone call from here in your study," McGuire offered, looking for all the world like a rebuked cocker spaniel. "But I don't know to whom she spoke or what was said. I didn't listen in on the conversation."

"You picked a damned poor time to turn over a new leaf."

Tugging at his ear, McGuire peered at him from beneath the sweep of ginger-colored lashes. A guilty smile split his face from ear to ear. "It was the sweetbreads I was braising for my dinner, sir. They require pampering."

Worth waved off the necessity of hearing more.

"Yes, well . . . I did pick up your tuxedo from the cleaners, and I've all your things laid out in your room. I was wondering if there's anything else? Before I go?"

"Go?"

"You do remember you gave me the rest of the evening off?"

Actually, Worth had forgotten, and he didn't care for the reminder now. Back when he'd told McGuire about the extra time off, he'd anticipated a wholly different scenario—one that had him and Rocky stealing away from the banquet early, rushing home to make wild, abandoned love without having to worry that McGuire might show up at an inopportune moment. Hell, no, he didn't want to be reminded of what was now highly unlikely. But he did want to find out why Rocky had changed her schedule.

"Yes, fine. Go then," Worth said, already on his way for the stairs.

He'd never climbed more quickly or felt a greater anxiety. If she was ill, it was all his fault. To add so much pressure to her life, especially with finals starting on Monday.

The door of her room was open. So was his. Wondering what was going on, he was totally unprepared when she rushed out of his doorway.

"Oh!" Skidding to a stop, she pressed a hand to her chest. "I didn't hear..."

"McGuire said..."

They stood a conservative three feet apart and stared at each other. Worth's initial reaction was helpless fascination. Rocky's was a mixture of things—anxiety, uncertainty and caution.

She was wearing the one-shouldered gown he'd purchased for her during their first shopping trip. How was it possible that, even barefoot, she could look more incredible in it now than when she'd first modeled it?

"I wanted to check in your mirror to see if it still looked okay," she explained after a small eternity. "I've gained some weight."

Pounds she needed, distributed in the most flattering places. Worth's heart beat a strong message against his chest. "You needn't explain or apologize. I—you're planning to go with me?"

"Maybe I shouldn't have presumed you'd want me to." She forced a smile. "But I remembered you saying how you disliked attending those things and absolutely hated going alone."

"I wouldn't go at all if it wasn't W.H. being honored, and important for business." Fool, he thought, that wasn't what he'd wanted to say. He *should* have said he was touched she'd remembered, ashamed that he hadn't checked with her before this, that she still took his breath away...

"Are you sure you're up to this?" was all he could manage. "I'm not, er, unaware that there's no love lost between you and my father."

"I'm not going for his sake."

Worth inclined his head, because no adequate words of gratitude formed in his head.

"Don't you think you'd better get ready yourself? It's getting late."

"Yes. I'm going."

But she was the one who moved. As she started for her room, Worth knew he owed her something more. A great deal more. "Rocky." When she stopped, waited, he murmured, "You look lovelier than ever."

No smile warmed her eyes or blossomed on her face. "Thank you. I'm glad you feel your investment has paid off."

Rocky didn't want to think about her cruelty. She'd meant to speak from the heart. Besides, Worth had all but put the words in her mouth himself, considering the boundaries he'd reestablished between them. That she spoke to him at all should seem like a gift to him.

She'd been in this place before—holding on to her world with chipped fingernails. It had been the norm when she'd been struggling to make a life for herself and Badger. She'd hoped, believed that with Worth she would never have to experience it again. It just went to show that living in an ivory tower didn't necessarily make one safe, even if the prince told you that you were.

"Be careful for what you ask, you might get it." That quote, newly learned, had been the theme of her existence for the past week, ever since Worth had redefined their relationship and thrust it back into its original perspective. Pride had demanded she not let him see how deeply that had wounded her, but it was taking every bit of her concentration to keep from letting pain and old fears consume her.

Slightly over an hour later, as she sat beside Worth at the front-row-center table facing the dais where W.H. and the guest speakers were seated, she knew that outwardly she appeared to fit in. Her gown was every bit as elegant as those of the mayor's wife seated across from her or the wife of the organization's president, the only other woman at the table. Rocky was also confident that she hadn't once used the wrong piece of silverware during the four-course meal. What's more she'd earned a nod of admiration from the mayor, seated on her right, during a discussion about zoning policies and how they hurt the poor in the city. But it was Worth's words ringing in her ears that kept her feeling like an impostor.

"Don't confuse my wanting you with anything more."

No, no matter how polite everyone at the table had been to her, she was certain they all saw her as merely Worth's mistress. It left an unpleasant taste in her mouth, and no matter how many sips of water she took from her crystal glass, it wouldn't be washed away. It didn't matter that she'd given herself to him for the best reasons. She'd lost her credibility. Her dignity. Worse, her identity. She wasn't sure how long she could hang on, but she needed to try.

Finals were next week. Once that was behind her, she would move out of Worth's house. To go where, she wasn't sure yet. Right now all her plans, not to mention her goals, were in a state of upheaval, and all she could make herself concentrate on was getting through exams.

She knew, however, that right afterward she would have to find a job. Juggling that responsibility along with classes intimidated her, but there was no way around it. At least she could take comfort in knowing she was now qualified to reach for something that paid more than minimum wage.

Chase caught her eye and winked. She understood his message; her mask of control was slipping. Dear Chase. As the master of ceremonies rose, she mouthed a thank-you across the table.

In the next instant Worth reached over and covered the hands she'd clasped in her lap with one of his. Startled, she shot him a quick glance. He didn't take his eyes off the speaker giving the opening remarks. The set of his jaw and the glint in his eyes, however, told her that he'd caught her exchange with Chase and didn't like it one bit.

She thought she would feel anger; instead she only knew sorrow. Yes, she thought with slow realization, it was sad to love someone who couldn't love you back, someone who only saw you as a possession to be coveted.

For the rest of the evening, Rocky forced herself to remain seated and still, despite wanting desperately to run away and hide. Speech followed speech, some better than others, but she clapped for all of them, while trying to emotionally distance herself from the scene. And through it all Worth stroked his thumb back and forth across her hand.

He couldn't stop. His annoyance over Chase's blatant flirting with Rocky had instigated the action, true, but Worth continued the contact because of a growing panic, one he wasn't quite sure he understood or would be willing to explain if he did. As a result he couldn't bring himself to look at her for fear that she would see the conflict in his face.

He barely heard any of the speeches, including his father's. When the last of the applause was over and the mass exodus began, Worth used the opportunity to assist

Rocky from her chair, then took her arm to keep the sea of shifting bodies from putting distance between them. Although he could sense her confusion in his behavior, even some unease, she didn't pull away from him.

"Well, how did I do?" W.H. asked, when the family reunited in the lobby of the hotel. His strong-featured face bore the signs of a rampant adrenaline surge. "Danvers tells me this is the best turnout they've had for one of these farces since their inception."

"Understandable," Chase drawled, rocking back on his heels. "Everyone figured out they wouldn't get another chance like this before your funeral."

An uneasy hush fell over the group until Rocky spoke up. "Congratulations, Mr. Drury. You handled the situation with far more grace than I'm sure many people would have."

W.H. barely spared her a glance and hailed someone behind her. Worth could almost feel her embarrassment, but it was nothing to the fury he experienced at his father's unacceptable behavior.

Perhaps W.H. had made it clear he disapproved of Worth's arrangement with Rocky. He could even be right that it was sheer lunacy for a man his age to become so involved with someone as young, as unworldly, but most of all someone from an economic and social background so innappropriate that it invited innuendo from the media and snubs from their social circle. Maybe he'd even misjudged Rocky to where he'd made himself a candidate to be financially taken to the cleaners. But that didn't excuse such callous behavior in public.

"Damn you, Worth," Chase muttered, "if you don't say something, I will."

"This is my responsibility," he replied. "Stay out of it."
Then refocusing on his father, he said, "I think Rocky just
complimented you, sir."

As his father stared at him seemingly befuddled, Rocky
said, "It doesn't matter."

He didn't dare look at her. The entreaty in her voice, the
embarrassment told him more than he wanted to know. "It
does to me. Father?"

He never called W.H. *Father.* Way back when, the old
man had announced that it sounded unprofessional because their personal lives would inevitably bleed into their
working lives so thoroughly. But for a moment the word
sounded right on Worth's lips.

It seemed to affect his father, as well. "Why, I didn't—
Well, I'm not sure I—I didn't actually hear..."

"A simple thank you would be sufficient, and then we'll
be leaving. Rocky has exams next week and she's been
burning the candle at both ends as it is. She needs her
rest."

W.H.'s silver eyebrows bobbed up and down. "Er, yes.
Of course. I must have been...thank you, my dear,
for...for taking time out to share this evening with me.
And good luck on your..."

Apparently Rocky had heard more than enough. With
a soft, terse "Excuse me," she bolted for the main exit.

"Way to go, bro," Chase muttered. "You could have let
everyone excuse the old man's snub as poor hearing. But
you had to rub everyone's nose in it."

Casting his brother a warning look, Worth took pur-
suit. The crowd was thinning. Nevertheless, he didn't catch
up with Rocky until he was outside.

She stood behind one of the steel pillars, trying to protect herself from the fine spring drizzle that had begun to
fall. Worth gave his ticket to one of the parking atten-

dants and approached her with as much care as if she was a cornered animal.

Her eyes were huge and vulnerable in the stark, artificial light. Stopping an arm's length away, he looked at her, looked up at the ugly lights and felt…too much. But how did you throw away thirty-six years of indoctrination? What did you cast off, and what did you keep?

"Are you all right?"

"Ask me twenty years from now. Maybe by then I can afford getting philosophical."

"If it's any comfort—"

"It won't be, so please don't waste your breath."

"Rocky."

He didn't know he could sound so…desperate. But with the throbbing echo pulsating in his ears, Worth stepped closer. His head filling with the scent of her shampoo, her hurt, their problems, he touched her hair and sighed.

"Don't. I can't breathe when you're this close," she whispered, turning away.

"And I hate it when you fight me."

"This isn't about you, I'm fighting me."

"Why?"

Her laugh was short and harsh. "To survive."

"Stop it."

"No!"

It was an intense, disturbing conversation to be having at the worst of all times. About to sacrifice words for action, Worth was stopped as the front doors of the hotel slid open again and a new batch of people poured out. In the same instant a screech of brakes sounded his car's arrival. Rocky shot away from the pillar and aimed for the car. She was inside before Worth had tipped the attendant.

Worth followed, his mood grimmer than ever. Resenting her control, and his lack of it, he raced off hotel property and attacked the streets like an ambulance driver. He expected the flash of red and blue lights behind him at any moment. Instead, about a mile away from the hotel, a small, muddy dog darted out from the darkness and cut across the beams of his headlights.

The horrific vision was too much like the phantom memory of events past. With a sound of denial locked in his throat, Worth hit the brakes.

"Oh, God. Worth," Rocky cried. "Stop!"

He expected a terrible impact. It didn't happen. Either his reflexes were better this time, or the mongrel had a guardian angel working overtime tonight. In any case, the mutt survived, merging with the darkness and leaving Worth and Rocky alone to recover in a shaky silence.

Feeling like a pressure cooker about to explode, Worth made a sharp right into the entrance of a deep, shrub-lined driveway of a remote estate. Surrounded by the twin walls of some overgrown evergreen, he braked again. When the car jerked to a halt, he shifted into park, killed his lights and struggled to ignore his trembling hands.

"What are you doing?" Rocky asked. "This is private property. The owners will think you're a burglar and phone the police."

"There's no one at home. I know the owners. They're in Bermuda for the yacht races. As long as we stay away from the front gates, we won't activate the cameras and alarms."

Rocky seemed reassured and slumped back in her seat. For a few, not-unpleasant seconds silence reigned. Then she murmured, "I heard a thump. Did you hit your head?"

Her voice had taken on that huskier sound that spoke of awareness, but it remained unsteady, too.

"No. My elbow. On the door. It's nothing." He knew he was back to sounding like the monosyllabic idiot he'd been before, but he couldn't seem to stop. "You?"

"I didn't hit anything, if that's what you mean."

"But you're not okay."

"Can't we just go back to the house?"

"Why?" Fear didn't allow him to be too generous. "So you can make a mad dash to your room and put a locked door between us?"

"What do you expect?" she cried, her temper rising. "After what you said to me?"

"Would you have preferred a *lie?*" he demanded, as cold as he'd ever felt.

"I would prefer never having met you!"

She couldn't mean that. She *didn't* mean that.

Furious, aggrieved, Worth yielded to the tumultuous feelings raging within him and unbuckled his seat belt, then hers, and dragged her across the car.

He thought he intended only to shake sense into her, to make her take back the ugly words. Never mind that he knew he deserved them. He wanted them obliterated. But touching her released all kinds of memories and feelings. There was no place to hide. No choice but to accept, to go with the blinding rush.

"Damn you," he groaned, hauling her closer. "Damn you!"

He couldn't find her mouth fast enough. When he did, it was like locking onto a live electrical outlet. Excitement exploded within him, and his body went stiff, hard with the energy that had slowly been sucking out of him over this past week. He tightened his hold and sought more.

"Worth, this isn't what you want," she murmured, trying to free herself.

"Yes it is. It's what we both want, the problem is we're too stubborn to admit it. Kiss me, Rocky."

"I can't let you..."

"Kiss me."

Trapping her between his shoulder and the car seat, he crushed his mouth to hers. He wasn't gentle, and neither was she as she fought to avoid his plunder. They went at each other with their entire bodies, oblivious or maybe not caring that their surroundings limited them severely and made injury inevitable, until Worth had her legs trapped in the crushing vise of his, and her hands imprisoned between their heaving chests.

Gasping for breath, Worth groaned against her mouth, "God, don't fight me. Damn it, Rocky, don't. Don't." At the first hint that she was listening to him, he kissed her cheek. "Help me."

In the vague, mysterious light from the dashboard, he waited for her eyes to open, for their gazes to collide. When she relented, the power of the moment reverberated through every inch of his body. A similar tremor rushed through hers. As a faint sound broke from her lips, her fingers uncurled. Then she gripped the lapels of his jacket and pulled herself even closer to him. Like a starving man, Worth locked his mouth to hers and feasted.

On some level he knew this was wrong. He knew he was taking advantage of a weak moment. But whose?

Twisted clothes complicated everything and yet made it more exciting. So was each shallow breath colliding, blending...burning, creating a new form of stimulation and torment, building on the most primitive urges to possess.

His hands obeyed the drive of his greed. They raced to mold her breasts, her waist, the long length of her sleek legs, to relearn the wonder of her, the perfect fit of their bodies. As he lowered his head to the cool, flawless skin on her shoulder, she trembled and writhed against him.

"It's been too long," he whispered, desire searing him. "I want to see you. Touch you."

"Worth, this is..."

"Yes, I know." Nothing had ever been more insane. "But we have to. Here. Now."

Yielding to the urgency to see her again, he dragged her gown off her shoulder, lower until he could reach the closures on her bra and released them, too. Then he protected her from the brisk, damp night air with his feverishly hot kisses.

With a cry, Rocky let her head fall back, surrendering to him, to anything he would give and take.

Passion filled the car with a steamy heat, further insulation against the night and reason. Desire sweetened it, softening the sharp, hard corners of the cramped car.

Finally loosening their clothes adequately, Worth felt desperation take on a momentum all its own. Already close, he lifted her over him again, drew her hips down, and felt his heart stop, swell, fill as she took him.

How hot, dewy, *tight* she was. With a groan, he clasped her close, closer, until he'd buried himself as deep as possible.

At that moment he would have sworn he could feel every cell in his body and hers. Surrounded by her, basking in her, he pushed, urged her to lean back and then pressed his mouth between her breasts. Beautiful, beautiful, he thought thrusting his hips against hers.

Her short nails bit into the tense cords of his neck, into his scalp, and her heart thudded frantically against his lips, telling him what he couldn't find words to ask. Responding to her whimpered plea, he frantically shifted his hold once more, urging her to follow the pagan rhythm he'd begun. And he whispered—dark, delicious, decadent things he'd never dreamed of saying to anyone before.

But this wasn't just anyone. This was the woman who had filtered through his defenses like a phantom, buried herself deep inside him, deeper than he was now buried in her. No matter how hard he tried to keep her locked out, her name was the whisper in every beat of his heart.

As the tremors of her ecstasy surrounded him and vibrated through him, Worth crushed Rocky close and gave himself up to his own shuddering release.

Rocky stayed in the cocoon of sensation for as long as she could. Even when she opened her eyes, she stayed protected from the night and total reality by the steam from their passion fogging the inside of the windows and the mist marbling on the outside. She refused to think about what a fool she'd been to participate in this, and that it only made her more vulnerable to more hurt down the road. She felt healed and full and, if not *needed*, then very, very much desired.

"I won't apologize," Worth said quietly.

"You don't have to. Besides, one of the things I admire most about you is that you've never lied to me."

Worth sighed against her hair. "Don't say things like that. You're tying me in knots as it is."

Was she? Maybe so. "Why is that? Why do you fight this—what's between us—so hard?"

"Because I don't believe in it."

She tried to move away. He stopped her.

"Don't. Please. Listen to me a minute."

Rocky closed her eyes, wishing she'd never asked the question. What had she expected him to say?

"I'm *afraid* to believe in what there is between us, Rocky. I'm afraid to believe that what happens when we make love is anything more than a momentary aberration.''

"You're afraid to be hurt."

"I won't be hurt," he said with chilling conviction. Then something like a spasm of pain crossed his face. "But I can't make myself set you free, either. You're mine. Do you understand me? Mine."

As he drew her tightly against him again, Rocky trembled. From what? Passion or fear? And was what he'd told her hopeless? Who wasn't afraid of being hurt? But through time, patience...love, most people got over that fear.

Dare she risk it? Dare she stay and show Worth her love for him until he felt confident enough to remove that armor that forced him to be so rigid?

"Let's go home," he murmured, brushing her hair aside to press his mouth to her neck. "I want you again. Let's go home and let me make love to you properly."

As he found a particularly sensitive spot with his tongue, Rocky trembled again and whispered, "Yes."

But in her mind another small voice cried for caution. She was just too dazed by love to listen.

Nine

If Rocky thought getting through her exams would be difficult before, the added concerns over her relationship with Worth made the experience all the more stressful. But somehow she got through them.

Then came the wait for her grades. The day each was posted, she rose extra early to be among the first waiting for the results. She figured this way, if the news was bad, she could escape before too many people were witness to her humiliation.

The A she received on her English exam proved more of a relief than a surprise. Considering Worth's intensive tutorship, the pressure was on not to let him down with a B, rather than doubting an A was possible.

But from there on things got more difficult.

On the morning the last grades were to be posted, she had to make a detour and get a cup of coffee at the café.

Her nerves were so bad she'd barely gotten any sleep the night before and was paying for it now.

A paper cup of coffee in hand, she walked across the green to the red brick building that held her fate. Her thoughts grew more philosophical with every step.

No matter how she did on the math exam—her weakest of all subjects—she could be proud of herself. Badger would have said something like that. She missed him more today than she had for months; maybe because it was almost his birthday; maybe because this was a moment one should be able to share with family.

Worth had been kind. Every night he would massage the tension out of her neck and shoulders and hold her as they lay in bed, without making any sexual overtures.

Oh, jeez, Worth... What was she going to do about him? About them? Since the morning after the banquet, she'd been more confused than ever.

He was trying to change. Defending her to his father had been a big deal to her, but there was something about his behavior since that concerned her. She felt as though he was acting the way he was because he thought *she* wanted him to, not because *he* wanted to. The difference mattered.

College was supposed to make you smarter, she brooded, climbing the last set of stairs and entering the math and science building. So how come she didn't feel it?

The instructor was late. Students came and went. One of the few who stayed helped pass the time by producing a deck of cards. Rocky shared a few pointers about playing poker that Fat Louie had passed on to her.

Finally, just before noon, a cheer rose from the stairwell. The group crowded in around the bulletin board, and a moment later, Rocky was staring at her last grade.

She'd done it. Somehow she'd achieved a 4.0 average. She...the dropout, the rebel, the statistic from the wrong side of town.

This was something she had to share with Worth. If it hadn't been for him...well, she would tell him everything that was in her heart as soon as she saw him.

She had money for a cab, barely. If the driver didn't mind a modest, very modest, tip. And Worth wouldn't mind her stopping by at the office, surely. She was wearing a navy blazer over dress jeans—the only kind she'd been able to talk Worth into buying for her—and an Oxford shirt. She looked presentable and would only stay a moment.

The cab was more like Cinderella's pumpkin before it had turned into a grand carriage, but Rocky didn't mind. She was concentrating on the view, anyway.

The sun had never seemed brighter, the city more friendly, the historic buildings less remote. My city, she thought, my home. And for the first time in her life, she believed it.

Drury Development was in the heart of the business district, in a more modern tower just south of Faneuil Hall. The uniformed guard at the information and security desk was helpful in directing her to the correct elevator, and once she reached the correct floor, the receptionist pointed out which hallway led to the executive wing. But once there, Rocky met an unexpected hindrance in the form of Worth's secretary.

A discreetly made up woman who dressed in pastels to match her soft silver hair made it clear that *Mr.* Drury was in a meeting and couldn't be disturbed.

"I don't mind waiting," Rocky replied with a quick smile.

"I don't believe you understand, miss. Mr. Drury sees no one without an appointment."

"He'll see me."

The woman's look told her she didn't believe her.

"We're...friends," Rocky added, hoping that would be enough of an explanation.

A slight flicker of speculation lit the woman's eyes, but she seemed to dismiss it just as quickly. "Perhaps there's something *I* can do for you."

So it was going to be like that, was it? Biting back the retort she might have given the woman a few months ago, Rocky matched the woman smile for smile. "There is. You can tell Mr. Drury that Rocky is here."

"Rocky!"

Rocky spun around, thrilled to hear a welcoming voice. "Chase! What a relief."

"So it would seem." Upon reaching her, Chase bent and kissed her cheek. "Problem?"

"Only that I can't get in to see Worth. Apparently it'd be easier getting an audience with the president."

Chase grinned and tapped the tip of her nose, "Honey, he *is* the president."

Rocky gaped. "Are you serious? I thought that was W.H."

"Chairman of the board."

"Oh, wow."

He uttered an exuberant laugh, the sound creating a wonderful wave of reaction with the other secretaries up and down the hall. "You're terrific, do you know that? You're exactly what this museum needs." Slipping his arm around her shoulders, he led her to the door of Worth's office. "Come on. I'll entertain you until he finishes his Sermon on the Mount."

"Mr. Drury," Worth's secretary warned. "I don't think—"

"It's on my head, Vivecca."

"We all have dreams, sir."

With a wicked wink, Chase nudged Rocky into Worth's office and quickly shut the door behind them. "Don't mind Vivecca. She's just been around Worth for too long."

"That's bad, Chase."

"Listen, you have to allow me my moments, or I'd go stark raving mad around here." He rubbed his hands together. "So, what brings you to the hallowed halls?"

It took Rocky a moment to answer. First she wanted to take in the place where Worth spent so much of his time and energy. Her initial reaction was that if she'd met him here instead of the way she did, she might never have become his lover.

There was no denying the beauty of the place. Slate gray fabric that looked like bamboo shades covered three walls. The fourth was all glass, giving him a view of more steel and glass and sky. A black couch stood in the center of the room, two cranberry red chairs faced it, and in between was a rectangular slab of glass balanced on twin pillars of black marble.

More degrees and awards covered the walls than pictures. And there were more books. But no novels, she concluded, circling the room and reading titles. This was the room of a tactician, a planner, a man who painstakingly structured and controlled the world around him. A room that evoked a persona that was even more powerful than the Worth *she'd* come to know.

It frightened Rocky.

"Don't take it too seriously, sweetheart," Chase murmured, from behind her. "It's all for show. Magicians use illusions, and in his own way, Worth's a master, too. I doesn't necessarily have anything to do with who he really is."

"Doesn't it?"

Chase drew a long breath and turned her around to face him. He slipped his hands into the pockets of his pale gray suit pants. "Maybe at one time it could have been. But you're changing him."

Rocky wanted to believe that. Then her gaze settled on his desk and she saw it.

As though drawn by a magnet, she crossed the room. On the left corner of the dark wood desk was a crystal statue, exquisite and romantic. Disturbing, too, because the figure was of a woman barely draped in some wispy veil. A young woman. A young woman with waist-long hair she was lifting off her neck the way...

"My God. It *is* me."

"So you can see the similarity, too."

"Who wouldn't? This is the piece you were referring to the day we met, isn't it?" she asked inching toward it. She hadn't forgotten; in fact, she'd searched for it at Worth's house, but without success. Eventually she'd let the matter go. After all, so much else had been going on at the time.

With no background whatsoever to qualify her hunches, Rocky could only guess about the artist who'd done this piece and what had inspired him. No doubt he'd been a dreamer—or else someone obsessed with his model. Surely no real person could possess the same qualities of innocence and wisdom, shyness and wantonness rendered by this figure? But if someone had convinced himself otherwise, pity the poor soul who had to try to live up to such expectations.

Pity her?

Rocky took a step back from the desk. An inner queasiness reminded her of the strong black coffee that lay on an otherwise empty stomach.

Was this why Worth had taken her into his home and under his wing? Had he intended to made her his mistress all along? Besides allowing herself to forget about that day in the gallery, she'd also let herself be convinced that Worth's generosity had been a result of feeling guilty for almost killing her.

"I want permission to lock my bedroom door."

"If you don't, I will."

"You're mine, Rocky. Mine."

The look on her face must have been frightening. Suddenly Chase was at her side and drawing her away from the piece. "Whatever you're thinking, don't. Damn, I should never have brought you in here without—"

"Hiding her?" Rocky smiled bitterly. "What does he call her, Chase?"

"C'mon, Rock. Cut yourself some slack."

"Tell me."

"Galatea."

"Pretty. Is she some goddess or something?"

"There're a few versions of her story in Greek mythology, but the most popular is that she was the statue that came to life when her owner, Pygmalion, the King of Cyprus, embraced her."

"I see," she murmured, her voice sounding to her as though she was speaking in a long, hollow tunnel. "Guess she was the old-fashioned rendition of the boy toy, huh?"

Chase shook his head, and placing a hand under her chin, forced her to meet his gentle eyes. "Let it go. Whatever his motivation in the beginning, I'm certain Worth has deeper feelings about you now. Listen," he said in a lighter tone, "you never told me what brought you here."

"It was going to be a...surprise." But that was back when she'd believed that Worth deserved to be the first one to share her good news with her. Back when she'd believed he was merely a strong man afraid of letting his heart direct his head. Back when she'd begun to believe in fairy tales and miracles.

What an idiot she'd proved herself.

She shut her eyes. "It's no big deal, really. I just wanted him to know that I'd gotten my last exam grade. That I'd done it, I made a perfect 4.0 av-av..."

"Ah, jeez, honey. Don't." Chase folded her into his arms and laid his cheek on the top of her head. "That's great news and I'm super proud of you."

It helped, being in his arms, knowing his sincerity was real and that it had no price. He might not be quite as tall as Worth or as muscular, and she wasn't in love with him the way she loved his brother, but Rocky clung tight, grateful for his strength and support.

She didn't actually hear one of the side doors open, she heard voices and felt Chase stiffen. Knowing what she would see, she eased out of his arms and turned to find Worth standing in the doorway of what looked to be a boardroom.

He said nothing, but his expression spoke volumes. At any other time she would have been hurt, even afraid. But for the moment at least, bitterness and anger protected her.

"Rocky came to give you some fantastic news," Chase said, in the heavy silence.

"Did she?"

"Never mind, Chase," she said. "It doesn't matter now."

"The heck it doesn't." Visibly frustrated, Chase turned to his brother. "She did it, man. She made it through with a perfect 4.0 average, and she came straight here to share the news with you. Unfortunately, seeing your prize possession over there has put a tarnish on the afternoon.''

An expert at understatement, Worth shut the boardroom door behind him. ''I can see you've come to some conclusions.''

At least, she thought, he did her the courtesy of not drooling over the object of discussion. ''Don't worry. I'll spare you most of them. Heck, I'll shelve all of them, except to say, shame on you, Worth. Shame on you for not coming straight out in the beginning and saying you were in the market for a life-size version of your dream woman!''

''It wasn't like that and you know it.''

''I don't know anything, except that you lied when you said you didn't want an affair, when you pretended to keep me at arm's length, when you—'' Hearing the tremor in her voice, she pressed her lips together, studied her jogging shoes and willed herself not to lose it. ''How could you take my dreams, my *heart* and manipulate it as though I was one of your... your projects!''

She wanted to scream. She wanted him to tell her that she was wrong. She wanted him to come to hold her and tell her that he loved her. Needed her. She prayed for him to swear she meant more to him than his fantasy over a pretty piece of glass.

He only shut his eyes. ''Chase,'' he said, his voice so low it was barely audible. ''Would you please leave us?''

''No, allow me,'' she snapped, already on her way to the door.

''Rocky, wait!'' Worth swore. ''All right then, I'll be home as soon as I cancel the rest of my—''

''Don't bother,'' she flung back at him. ''I won't be there!''

* * *

"You've had a bad time of it."

One week later, Rocky sat in the loft Danielle Lanier called home and hugged her knees to her chest. Across from her Dani sat on a half-stripped rocking chair, knitting furiously at what had to be the longest scarf in the world.

"No worse than anyone else," Rocky said, eyeing the ugly orange thing and wondering. "Did I shock you when I confessed to being Worth's mistress?"

The needles went still, and gentle cat green eyes gazed at her without judgment. "You were his lover. There's a difference. And for the record, nothing shocks me. Like you, I can't afford to let it. If I did, I couldn't survive half of what I've seen. If you and Worth Drury had a relationship, then it was because he showed you a side of himself that deserved taking a risk on. I'm sorry it didn't work out. I'm angry as *hell* that he did such a hatchet job on your self-esteem."

Although warmed by the support, Rocky was surprised at Dani's vehemence. After all, the kids at the hostel had a reason for calling the redhead St. Dani behind her back. "I'm also a bit put out that you didn't come to me that first night," Dani continued, back to rocking and knitting.

Rocky had spent the first two nights at the hostel, and when Worth almost succeeded in tracking her down, she'd spent the next few nights in any corner she could find. When Dani heard about that, she'd immediately brought her here.

"You'll stay with me, and you'll continue with school immediately," she'd said in that soft but firm voice that accepted no argument. "At least one class."

"First I have to find a job," Rocky cautioned.

"You have a job. You're now my assistant. I've watched you for some time," Dani explained, "and I see your gift for handling people, especially the kids around here. I need you, Rocky. This is no gesture of charity."

It had been that simple, and if it wasn't for her heartbreak, Rocky would have been thrilled with her new prospects. Focusing on her new boss helped her forget herself.

Life hadn't turned Dani bitter, despite her own tragedies. Rocky wished she knew her secret.

"There's no secret," the eccentric social worker replied. "Just faith, and a strong stubborn streak that doesn't let me give up—especially when things look their worst. Believe me, I've been in such dark places, there was nowhere to go but up."

Rocky couldn't picture it. Not Dani. "Has there ever been anyone . . . ?"

"Special?"

Embarrassed for sounding nosy, Rocky nodded. "Half the boys in the hostel have a crush on you."

"Half the boys in the hostel still need mothers," her new roommate pointed out with a dry smile. Then she grew somber. "Okay, honesty time. I suffer from extreme tunnel vision. Someone would really have to be a charmer to make me notice him, and I'm afraid there aren't that many white knights around in the circles I travel."

Bemused, Rocky murmured, "What if I told you there was someone interested in meeting you? Kind of like an admirer from afar?"

"I'd say, I'm going to shove this useless stress therapy into my knitting box and put some popcorn into the microwave. Then I'll show you my files. In other words, one broken heart in this household at a time is enough."

Having a support unit like Dani was a new experience to Rocky. It made tolerating the pain of leaving Worth almost bearable. It also gave her strength to admit it was perfectly understandable to feel a new wave of hurt when he stopped looking for her.

As time passed and one month became two, then two became three, her anger with him turned to sorrow. How could she miss someone who had hurt her so deeply? her rational mind would argue. Her answers were slow to show themselves.

She missed him for his brilliant financial mind when a broker came snooping around Dani's building and tried to scare her into selling the property. She missed him for his lectures on patience and decorum countless times, when the unavoidable necessity for solicitations earned her a variety of snubs. She missed him for his ability to make even her boring homework interesting.

And she ached for his lovemaking. At night she dreamed he came to her, undressed her and rained kisses down her body the way he used to when he was out late for a meeting and she'd collapsed in bed, exhausted from studying.

Regardless of his manipulations, she knew that in walking away from him, she'd lost a vital part of her life. Regardless of the problems, maybe the complex, disturbing things that had torn them apart, Worth had picked her up by the scruff of the neck and forced her to face the world head-on and not settle for getting by. For that she could never bring herself to leave him out of her prayers.

Unlike Worth, Chase refused to keep his distance. He proved an excellent friend: offering money, which she refused—except as a donation to Dani's agency; room and board in his own apartment, which earned him a kiss on the cheek; and an offer to argue her case with Worth, which she adamantly turned down.

Eventually he settled for the right to visit her now and then, either offering his services as a referee for some field game at the hostel, a strong back wherever it was needed or an adviser for locating new contributions.

Of course, Rocky wasn't so naive not to notice that whenever he was around, his gaze searched for Dani. Unfortunately Dani seemed barely conscious of him.

"Am I wasting my time?" Chase asked Rocky one afternoon in September as he drove her home from class. "She doesn't seem to mind me visiting you."

"She knows you've been a good friend and a help to Heaven Can Wait."

"But when I've asked her out, she's done everything but laugh at me."

"Dani doesn't laugh at people. She respects feelings too much."

"You sound smitten yourself, Rock. What I need are answers. Facts."

It pained Rocky to supply them. "You have a reputation, Chase. She reads the paper, even the society columns. She has to, in order to keep up with potential contributors for her programs. I've tried to let her know that you're trying to turn over a new leaf."

"Trying?" Chase's face turned red. "For the first time in my life I meet someone I want to approach seriously, someone I want to convince of my sincerity, and you summarize it as *trying* to turn over a new leaf? I'll bet she was impressed."

"She's cautious, Chase. Cautious women don't leap blindly into relationships like the rest of us."

Immediately he blanched and reached across the car to squeeze her shoulder. "I'm sorry, honey. If it's any consolation he's still not seeing anyone, either."

Despite the embarrassment of having him know she refused to date, Rocky had to ask, "Does he ever...mention me?"

"Not in words. But if it's any consolation, he looks like garbage. What's more, W.H. has to raise heck to get him to do any after-hours socializing for the firm. All he wants to do these days is to go back to that dungeon of his and mope."

Her vulnerability over hearing that news forced her to mutter, "He's never going to find his living and breathing *Galatea* that way."

"Maybe he thinks he found someone even better."

Rocky felt a pain in her heart that was difficult to hide, but she forced herself to keep her gaze straight ahead. "I thought you said he wasn't dating?"

"I did."

"Then what are you talking about?" she demanded tightly.

"You have to figure that out for yourself."

Fall was like one long shower without warm water. Worth thought it matched his mood perfectly. By late November he was in such a dismal mood that he avoided Thanksgiving dinner at his father's by pleading a case of the flu. Considering that his father knew damned well he hadn't even had a cold in nearly five years, he wasn't surprised that it spawned an eruption on the following Monday, right after the morning executive meeting.

"This crap has to stop, boy!"

"Has my job performance suffered?" Worth asked, staring out the window of his office.

"You know damn well it hasn't, but the instant it does, the board—"

"Can do what they please. In the meantime they can mind their own business, and you can do the same."

"That's a helluva way to talk to your father," W.H. growled, showing his agitation in the way he fidgeted with things on Worth's desk.

Worth watched his reflection in the window. Age was creeping up on the old man, but at the moment he couldn't let it matter. "You've managed to forget our blood ties for the better part of thirty years in exchange for creating a partner. You're asking for a lot to ask for special treatment now."

"Maybe I am." W.H. tugged at his ear and scowled at Worth's desk. "What's different here?"

From one unwelcome subject to another. Worth sighed inwardly, wishing an emergency call would materialize so he could end this fiasco. "The sculpture is gone."

"So it is. Where'd it go?" W.H. glanced around, hunting for it.

"I took it to the house."

"Is it any replacement for her?" As Worth began to turn around, W.H. waved the remark away. "I wasn't being crass, I'm curious. Concerned, whether you believe me or not."

"You want something," Worth suggested, his glance droll.

"Yeah, my president with all his screws tightened." Shoving his hands into his pockets, W.H. slowly made his way around to stand beside Worth. "And to ask you to accept my apology."

"I thought you already did?"

"No, about . . . the girl. About the way I treated her."

Worth didn't want to talk about Rocky. It caused too much pain. Wasn't it enought that he had to go through every day knowing he wouldn't see her lovely face, hear her husky laugh, touch her sweet, lithe body? Did he have to be forced to talk about her, too?

"Maybe I wasn't as fair as I could have been toward her," W.H. continued, seemingly oblivious to Worth's silence. "I tried to convince myself that it was the age thing, but...well, she proved she could keep up with you, didn't she?"

Not meaning to do more than listen, Worth found himself facing his father and murmuring, "Go ahead."

"I was a snob. I had myself convinced she wasn't good enough for the family."

"We don't have a family, W.H., we have a corporation." But this time Worth managed a faint smile.

His father shrugged. "At least our arguments don't get as personal as they do in traditional families. Let me finish, will you? I want you to know that you have my blessings if you decide..."

"She doesn't want to be found."

"What are you talking about? Chase sees her all the time."

Oh, yes, he knew. Apparently *everyone* in this blessed place knew. "She doesn't want to be found by *me.*"

"And you're going to stand for that?"

"Yes. If that's what she wants. It's the only gift I can give her. Her freedom, her independence. She's earned it."

"I guess I never did understand the whole concept of love," W.H. muttered, shaking his head and heading for the door.

Worth turned back to the window. "And I learned too late."

They argued again. About the company Christmas party. For once Worth had slowed down long enough to listen to the rumblings of discontent in the office. Remembering how *he'd* left early last Christmas Eve, he agreed it was the wrong time for the celebration and talked his father into doing some fast and intensive coordinating, and holding it two weeks earlier. Then he tried to get out of attending.

"What are you talking about?" W.H. roared. "I did this for you, now you have to be there."

Worth studied the man who had sired him, then had missed his birth because of a meeting in Geneva; had missed his first steps because he'd been in Paris; and had missed a dozen other important hallmarks in his life due to trips to London, Berlin, New York and every other city where the scent of business deals had lured him. Worth could forgive, but he had a hard time forgetting. "Give me one good reason," he replied.

"You always give the 'thanks for a great year' speech before I hand out the bonus checks."

"So, you do it for a change."

"I want *you* to do it."

"Have Chase do it."

"Chase can't do it."

"Of course, he can. He inherited your gift for sugar-coated hyperbole."

"Blast it all, Chase is going to be late," W.H. shot back. "You want to know why he's going to be late?"

"Not particularly."

"You remember, you forced me. Chase is going to be late because he's bringing a guest. A special guest. And he swore me to secrecy, and now I've broken my word. Damn it, Worth, I've had enough of this whole business. I'm too old for this foolishness. You *be* there."

Ten

"Has Chase arrived yet?"

"Try to look as though you're having a good time, son."

"I thought you said—"

"He'll be here. You know what traffic is like during the holidays, especially at this hour."

Worth knew, but it didn't do anything for the acid that had been burning in his stomach ever since W.H. had told him that Chase was bringing someone to the party. He took a sip of his drink and tried to let the liquor soothe his nerves.

Was he setting himself up for disappointment? Chase had never said that Rocky would be his date, and Worth couldn't see her doing such a thing. Rocky wasn't a woman who would throw a new relationship in his face.

Worth forced himself to take a calming breath ... and grew increasingly heartsick. What if she didn't come? He'd spent the past several days imagining all the things he would say if she let him get close enough to her to say them. How would he get through the night if it turned out to be a bad joke on Chase's part?

No, even Chase had been almost sympathetic lately. The sarcasm that had underscored much of their relationship seemed to be gentler these days. Or was it an aberration of the season?

In a matter of days, two weeks to be exact, it would be Christmas. A year since he'd met her. In the several months they'd been apart each had experienced a birthday. For her it had been a major one, her twenty-first. He had missed helping her celebrate her "coming of age." Chase had done it for him, or so he'd heard from W.H.

"Maybe you want to do your speech before your brother gets here, in case things don't go as expected?" W.H. asked, leaning toward him.

What was it that he expected? he almost asked back. For the life of him he didn't know—except that he knew if he didn't at least see those midnight eyes again, he might go quietly out of his mind.

"Let's wait a few more minutes," he replied, scanning the room. "People have barely begun sampling the buffet, and—"

He forgot what else he'd been about to say because the front door swung open and he recognized Chase's blond head above the sea of people standing in between them. His heart pounding, Worth craned his neck to see who he was escorting inside. His palms grew damp. God, he thought, had he ever known such an agony?

Yes. The day she left you.

The wall of bodies parted and he saw . . . a redhead.

A strange disappointment surged through him. Because it was mixed with shock and relief, it wasn't as debilitating as he'd expected.

Who was she? She certainly looked intriguing—if hesitant. Two points for her, Worth thought, his bitterness returning. At least she appeared to have sense; she needed every bit of it if she intended to be around a Drury.

Then slowly anger surged through the muddle of his confusion. Where was Rocky? How could Chase treat her like this?

Redefining torture, Worth forced himself to wait for the couple to wade through the partygoers. He managed by concentrating on not splintering plastic and splashing liquor over himself and his employees. His father proved no help whatsoever.

"A redhead...Chase has never been out with a redhead before. I wonder if that means this could be serious?"

Finally Chase and his guest stood before them. "W.H., Worth...may I introduce Danielle Lanier. Dani to her friends, of which, I hope I'm now privileged to call myself one," he added with a gallant bow to his companion. "Dani, my father and—"

Before he could finish, Worth ground out, "How could you, Chase?"

"How could I what, bro?"

Worth glanced at his brother's date, who was eyeing him strangely. She had unusual eyes, and the emotions within them were disconcerting, as well. He was certain they'd never met before, and yet there was no denying she studied him with great curiosity, combined with a definite coolness. Considering that he would have initially described her face as angelic, it was an unsettling inspection from a stranger.

Giving himself a mental shake, he murmured, "Forgive me, Miss Lanier." Then he snarled at Chase, "Knowing how Rocky feels about you, how can you be this insensitive to her feelings?''

Startled, but recovering quickly, Chase slipped an arm around his date's waist and eyed his brother with unapologetic amusement. ''Well, I thought you of all people would figure it out, old boy. I'm keeping up with Drury tradition.''

It would have given Worth great satisfaction to wipe his brother's glib smile off his face, but he restrained himself. He did, however, curtly excuse himself and retreat to his office.

Shutting and locking the door behind him, but not bothering with the lights, he paced, swore and finally yielded to the emotions boiling within him. With a vicious curse he slammed his fist against the door to his washroom. It set off flashbulbs before his eyes, but did nothing to ease the anger and torment bubbling inside him.

Ah, Rocky . . . Rocky.

Too overwhelmed by the darkness, he went to the window.

Above the streetlights and buildings, the moon rose in a clear sky, magically, mockingly. As though he needed reminding of that other night last December, when once upon a full moon, fate had presented him with a gift he'd been too blind, too rigid to appreciate.

Rocky. To be hurt by yet another Drury. She didn't deserve this. He wanted to go to her, offer some comfort; but, he reminded himself, he was the last person she would want to see, let alone deliver such terrible news.

The darkness seemed to expand around him making his office, his life, close in on him. Suddenly he couldn't breathe, he couldn't think. Knowing he needed to get out, he grabbed his coat out of the closet and exited through his private door. W.H. would throw a fit when he discovered he'd been abandoned, but that couldn't matter.

Like someone running for his life, he hurried to the garage, every step feeling more weighted than the last. By the time he reached the garage, he thought he'd aged a decade.

His car suffered his brutal handling well and merged with the congestion on the streets like a great predator eager to take on any challenges. Around him the city hummed with Christmas shopping traffic, music and bells. Worth added a blast of his horn to the din, as a taxi cut in front of him. Shortly afterward he raced through a yellow light, desperate to leave the scene, the sounds, the joy behind him.

But he couldn't flee from his thoughts.

She would like the noise, the colors and euphoria the season brought. She would probably have convinced him that this was the year to try new things, to walk arm in arm and window-shop, once she'd learned he'd never done it before. Walk until their faces were frozen from the wind whipping off the bay and their feet were more numb than sore. He would have suggested a cappuccino at one of the tower restaurants, someplace dark and quiet with a pianist playing softly in the background. Or someplace where music was unnecessary because they had each other.

Oh, God, his mind was in rare form tonight.

He prepared himself for the turn at the next light, then tried not to look at the alley where she'd sprung from, the night she changed his life. He tried not to wish he had the chance to do it all over again.

"You're sick," he muttered with self-disgust.

Maybe, but he also knew he would do things differently this time. At least this time he would have had the sense not to blow it.

Second chances, however, weren't in the cards for him. Less than five minutes later he arrived at his home without any incident whatsoever.

Except that McGuire didn't meet him at the door as he usually did.

Worth struggled to remember, had he given the man the night off? Had he fired him? Maybe McGuire had had enough of his foul moods lately and had quit.

He let himself in and called his servant's name.

There was no answer, and the only light was from a painting lamp at the opposite end of the foyer.

"McGuire!" he shouted again, impatiently ripping off his coat and scarf. He tossed both over the stairs' banister. Hell, he fumed, if the man hadn't quit, he had a good mind to fire him.

With a heavy sigh he entered his study and headed straight for the bar. Hopefully the reprobate had thought to supply him with ice before taking off to heaven only knew where.

The ice was there, and Worth wasted no time in pouring himself a drink. Then, uncharacteristically, he swirled the frozen cubes in the amber liquid, so he could hear the tinkling of ice against crystal. It was a trait of Rocky's when she drank iced tea, a trait that used to drive him mad because she always seemed to do it when he was trying to concentrate on something.

He turned away from his thoughts and back to the room where the moonlight, filtering in through the sheer draperies, provided the only light. A mystical blue-white glow he'd come to favor when making love to Rocky, since it made her skin resemble alabaster and the highlights in her hair shine like Swiss blue topaz. Now it permeated the room, deepening shadows and giving energy to things like—

Worth's gaze froze on his desk.

Galatea. She was gone!

He'd put her there after deciding to remove her from his office. Her presence there had ceased to give him the pleasure she once did, and because he rarely worked in here these days it had seemed the appropriate exile for her. But to have her mysteriously vanish...

"Looking for something?"

His searching gaze found her in time to see the door shut. The lock was set. Worth's heart began slamming against his chest.

She stepped out of the darkness, seeming to glide as she moved toward him, a vision in an off-the-shoulder white gown that looked as substantial as morning dew against her slender body. In comparison, *Galatea* looked bland between her hands.

His mouth went dry, and there was a roaring in his ears. Certain he had to be dreaming, he willed himself to awaken and end the nightmare. Instead, ice clicked more forcefully in his glass.

This was no dream. He dropped, more than set, the crystal tumbler onto the desk. Some of the contents spilled onto the back of his hand, but he didn't care. He couldn't take his eyes off her.

"I said," she murmured, as she became fully spotlighted in a shaft of moonlight, "are you looking for something?"

He couldn't make his voice work. "I was."

"This?" She offered him *Galatea*.

He accepted the sculpture, but without taking his eyes off her. Setting it aside, he managed more firmly, "No. Something... some*one* more special. And rare. Someone who brought light and laughter into my life. Meaning.

Someone who turned my world inside out when she left me.''

"Why did she leave you?"

The voice that he remembered as part velvet, part whiskey, embraced him like a secret. "Because I was slowly, methodically destroying her, crushing everything unique and genuine about her. I thought I was doing her a favor by taking her out of the gutter and showing her utopia."

"Maybe you did."

"No. I didn't realize at the time that each of us carries our own utopia within us. It's not something you can buy for someone or will upon someone."

Worth bowed his head in shame. "I realized the perfect world she carried inside her, the things she called dreams, was also what triggered my fascination with her. Before I knew what was happening to me, I was obsessed with her. It was one thing to be infatuated with a piece of art, but entirely another when the center of your existence becomes another human being. Especially one so young, so inexperienced, so irreverent."

"You fought her."

"I fought myself. She scared the hell out of me, made me begin to want things I'd taught myself not to trust in. I thought, given the right opportunity, I could prove to myself that she would disappoint me. Why not? Up until her, everyone else had managed to."

"And she did disappoint you."

Hearing her voice tremble with sadness forced Worth to shake his head vehemently. "No! You did the only thing you could do to survive. I was still locked in my rigidity, unable to believe I could need. My determination to hang on to my addiction for control forced you away."

"Need?" she whispered, tears shimmering in her eyes as she locked on to that word.

Realizing how precious it was to her, Worth circled the desk. "Yes, *need*. Your energy and sweetness and courage. Rocky... you've become so strong and come so far." Hesitantly, as though fearing she might vanish before his eyes, he lifted a hand to her hair, skimmed the back of his fingers across her cheek, took gentle hold of her upper arms. "On the other hand, I've become the one in need of a tutor. I need someone to keep teaching me how to accept someone for who and what that person is, not for what I can turn them into."

He shut his eyes, seeing too much of his past, the pain he'd caused as a result of his autocratic manner and self-righteous sense of entitlement. "Is it too late for me, do you think?"

"It depends on what your goals are."

"I only have one." Taking courage from the emotions he saw warming her gem-bright eyes, Worth exposed her to his heart completely. "To love you with all that's within me. To spend the rest of my life showing you how much I adore you."

Then, with a groan, he gave in to the necessity of convincing himself she was real and drew her tightly against him. "Rocky... ah, God, Rocky."

Their first kiss was a tremulous communion that quickly escalated into a desperate searching; the urgency to experience again the pleasure and joy that could radiate between them very real. Butterfly kisses followed, sweetened by Rocky's own whispers of love. Then it was necessary to simply hold each other fast and relish the moment of being together.

"Dear Lord, I missed you." Worth inhaled the fresh, ready scent of her hair and rubbed his cheek again and again against its silky softness. "I can't tell you how many times I wanted to come after you. Apologize for trying to

suppress who you were instead of appreciating and en
couraging you. I wanted to beg you to forgive me. Plead
with you to give me another chance.''

"I know you did initially," she said, her smile sad. "But
why did you stop?''

"I realized I was only pushing you farther away by try
ing to chase you down.''

"Yes," Rocky admitted. "You were right. I needed
time, but at first I was hurt, and I thought it meant you'd
stopped caring.''

"Never.'' He kissed her again, wishing there was some
way to obliterate all of that from her memory. But he knew
only time could do that.

"Then I realized you'd given me the best of all pres
ents.'' Rocky smiled at his look of doubt. "Yes, it's true
because the freedom you gave me allowed me to test all
those things you'd taught me, and I matured. I don't think
anything else could have prepared me to be a better part
ner to you.''

It wasn't what he'd expected to hear, and impressed him
more than he thought possible. Sensing she had more to
say, he drew back and waited.

"You're not the only one who faced some doubts while
we were apart," Rocky continued. "I did, too. And,'' she
added, spreading her hands over his chest, as though
touching him was as important as getting these things said,
"I realized I had some of my own rigidness and precon
ceived notions to deal with. As I began working with Dani,
I quickly realized that I had a great deal more to learn from
you.''

"Dani?'' As flattering as her admission was, it was that
name that had Worth listening with even greater interest.

"Do you mean the redhead who showed up with Chase at the company party tonight?"

Rocky's smile grew impish. "The very same one who was with Chase when he dropped me off here, yes."

Beginning to believe in this miracle enough to relax, Worth teased, "So I was the victim of a conspiracy, hmm?"

"A hastily put together one."

Worth thought about how he'd attacked Chase, and he suffered a sharp pang of regret. "Remind me to apologize to my brother when we see him again."

"Oh, dear. That bad?"

"Bad enough. Although, now that I think about it, he took it all in stride. What did you do to McGuire after he let you in?" Worth asked, raising one of her hands and awarding each finger a suckling kiss. "Lock him in the pantry?"

With a soft laugh, Rocky shook her head. "I knew he would keep trying to cook for us, and I figured we wouldn't want to be thinking about food for several hours, so I gave him the night off. Do you approve?"

"I couldn't have delegated authority to a better judge of character," he said, laughing. But just as quickly he grew somber. "I love you, darling. Anything else you want to tell me before I start proving how much?"

Rocky slipped her arms around his neck and whispered, "Only that being away from you for these months has shown me how much I want to experiment with all that flexibility we've been learning about."

"What about a lifetime's worth?"

With a brief, brilliant smile she rose on tiptoe and gave him her lips for a kiss that made sure he had no doubts as to what her answer was. Worth shuddered as the last walls of reservation and doubt crumbled between them.

"This is what gave me the courage to come here tonight," she murmured. "The knowledge that when you love someone, you're only half-alive unless you're with them."

Worth tightened his arms around her. "Don't ever leave me again."

"Never."

"I need you, Rocky."

Raising her head, she corrected him impishly, "A dress like this requires a Roxanne."

Worth laughed, enjoying her spirit. "If we take it off, you can just be you—which is exactly what I want my wife to be."

"Worth..." As he reached to the back of her dress and began lowering the zipper, she trembled. "Are you sure? I couldn't bear it if you decided later that you might have made a mistake."

"The only thing I'll ever regret is that we didn't get you pregnant after that night in the car."

Mischief brought the sapphire lights back into her eyes. "Is this a good time to tell you that I stopped taking my birth control pills right after I moved out?"

"Oh...yes," Worth replied, drawing the silk away from her body.

Then he reached behind him and dropped it over the crystal statue. He didn't glance back to check his aim. As far as he was concerned, the rarest work of art was the one he was holding in his arms.

As they eagerly finished undressing each other and sank to the plush carpet, Worth gazed in wonder at the beauty of the woman he'd thought he'd lost forever. "Rocky...

there's one thing you'd better know. You'll always be my obsession."

"I'm not afraid of you using that word anymore," she whispered. "Because now you know there's an obsession that's born out of love. Let me show you."

And drawing him down to her, she did.

*   *   *   *   *

**Rugged and lean...and the best-looking,
sweetest-talking men to be found in the
entire Lone Star state!**

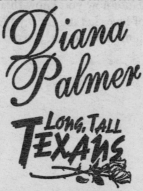

*Diana
Palmer*

LONG, TALL
TEXANS

In July 1994, Silhouette is very proud to bring you
Diana Palmer's first three LONG, TALL TEXANS.
CALHOUN, JUSTIN and TYLER—the three cowboys
who started the legend. Now they're back by popular
demand in one classic volume—and they're ready to
lasso your heart! Beautifully repackaged for this
special event, this collection is sure to be a
longtime keepsake!

"Diana Palmer makes a reader want to find a Texan
of her own to love!"   —*Affaire de Coeur*

**LONG, TALL TEXANS—the first three—
reunited in this special roundup!**

**Available in July,
wherever Silhouette books are sold.**

LTT

MILLION DOLLAR SWEEPSTAKES (III)

No purchase necessary. To enter, follow the directions published. Method of entry may vary. For eligibility, entries must be received no later than March 31, 1996. No liability is assumed for printing errors, lost, late or misdirected entries. Odds of winning are determined by the number of eligible entries distributed and received. Prizewinners will be determined no later than June 30, 1996.

Sweepstakes open to residents of the U.S. (except Puerto Rico), Canada, Europe and Taiwan who are 18 years of age or older. All applicable laws and regulations apply. Sweepstakes offer void wherever prohibited by law. Values of all prizes are in U.S. currency. This sweepstakes is presented by Torstar Corp., its subsidiaries and affiliates, in conjunction with book, merchandise and/or product offerings. For a copy of the Official Rules send a self-addressed, stamped envelope (WA residents need not affix return postage) to: MILLION DOLLAR SWEEPSTAKES (III) Rules, P.O. Box 4573, Blair, NE 68009, USA.

EXTRA BONUS PRIZE DRAWING

No purchase necessary. The Extra Bonus Prize will be awarded in a random drawing to be conducted no later than 5/30/96 from among all entries received. To qualify, entries must be received by 3/31/96 and comply with published directions. Drawing open to residents of the U.S. (except Puerto Rico), Canada, Europe and Taiwan who are 18 years of age or older. All applicable laws and regulations apply; offer void wherever prohibited by law. Odds of winning are dependent upon number of eligibile entries received. Prize is valued in U.S. currency. The offer is presented by Torstar Corp., its subsidiaries and affiliates in conjunction with book, merchandise and/or product offering. For a copy of the Official Rules governing this sweepstakes, send a self-addressed, stamped envelope (WA residents need not affix return postage) to: Extra Bonus Prize Drawing Rules, P.O. Box 4590, Blair, NE 68009, USA.

SWP-S594

SILHOUETTE® Desire®

SAXON BROTHERS

An exciting new trilogy from JACKIE MERRITT

You met Chance Saxon in WRANGLER'S LADY (D #841) and Rush Saxon in MYSTERY LADY (D #849).

Now don't miss PERSISTENT LADY (D #854), when determined Cash Saxon goes to the untamed wilderness of Oregon and meets his match in one *very* persistent woman!

Let the SAXON BROTHERS keep you warm at night—only from Silhouette Desire!

If you missed either of the first two books in THE SAXON BROTHERS series, *Wrangler's Lady* (D #841) or *Mystery Lady* (D #849), order your copy now by sending your name, address, zip or postal code, along with a check or money order (please do not send cash) for $2.99 for each book ordered, plus 75¢ postage and handling ($1.00 in Canada), payable to Silhouette Books, to:

In the U.S.	In Canada
Silhouette Books	Silhouette Books
3010 Walden Ave.	P.O. Box 636
P.O. Box 9077	Fort Erie, Ontario
Buffalo, NY 14269-9077	L2A 5X3

Please specify book title(s) with order.
Canadian residents add applicable federal and provincial taxes.

SDSAX3

CAN YOU STAND THE HEAT?

Silhouette™

SUMMER Sizzlers '94

You're in for a serious heat wave with Silhouette's latest selection of sizzling summer reading. This sensuous collection of three short stories provides the perfect vacation escape! And what better authors to relax with than

ANNETTE BROADRICK
JACKIE MERRITT
JUSTINE DAVIS

And that's not all....

With the purchase of *Silhouette Summer Sizzlers '94*, you can send in for a FREE Summer Sizzlers beach bag!

SUMMER JUST GOT HOTTER—
WITH SILHOUETTE BOOKS!

SS94

SILHOUETTE®

Desire®

Coming in May
from Silhouette Desire

When an

Irresistible!

man meets an unattainable woman...
sparks fly!

**Look for these exciting men in books
created by some of the top authors in
contemporary romance:**

#853	LUCY AND THE STONE by Dixie Browning (Man of the Month)
#854	PERSISTENT LADY by Jackie Merritt
#855	BOTHERED by Jennifer Greene
#856	A LAWLESS MAN by Elizabeth Bevarly
#857	ONCE UPON A FULL MOON by Helen R. Myers
#858	WISH UPON A STARR by Nancy Martin

Don't miss them—only from Silhouette Desire!

SDIRR